ALSO BY AMANDA HAMM

WEATHERING EVAN

THE 4ᵀᴴ FLOOR LOUNGE

MEET CUTE: 5 ROMANTIC SHORT STORIES

THE STORIES FROM HARTFORD SERIES
ANDREW'S KEY
JEALOUSY & YAMS
COLLECTING ZEBRAS
THE CHRISTMAS PROJECT
HEARTS ON THE WINDOW (EBOOK NOVELLA)

THE COFFEE AND DONUTS SERIES
SAID AND UNSAID
SOFIE WAITS
A PERFECTLY GOOD MAN
NOT COMPLICATED

THEY SEE A FAMILY
THE STUDY GROUP (EBOOK NOVELLA)

LOVE IN ANDAUK SERIES
EVERYTHING OLD

Into the Fire

Amanda Hamm

ISBN: 978-1-943598-10-6

Into the Fire is a work of fiction. All names, characters, places, events, etc. are products of the author's imagination or are used fictitiously.

1

What was Jillian doing in Andauk? That was a question Joseph had no intention of asking. He ducked into the nearest shop to avoid being seen. A tinny bell jingled as he entered, and a scent he hadn't encountered in years filled his nose. It smelled like a mix of dust and cleaning products. Weird.

Joseph ignored the smell as the old woman who owned Granny's Shelf appeared before him. He knew she hadn't just appeared. She came from behind a shelf. But he hadn't seen her through the glass shelves lined with mostly glass knickknacks, and her footsteps were oddly quiet. She was standing in front of him pretty suddenly.

"Can I help you?" she asked. Her thin lips formed a friendly smile. She'd looked old when he was a kid but the lines on her face seemed unchanged after twenty or so years.

"I, uh, just wanted to look around for a bit." Just because he didn't say why he wanted to look around didn't make it any less true. His footsteps echoed in the silent store and made him want to slow his pace. The vibrations, however slight, didn't seem healthy to the fragile surroundings.

The old woman was short and thin. Physically, she seemed very frail. But her eyes and mind were missing nothing as she watched him move along the shelf. The silence made him tense. He couldn't think of anything to say. *You sure have a lot of glass stuff. Don't you want to put on some music or something? These shelves are spotless. Where is the dust smell coming from?* Perhaps he could think of things to say, but he wasn't going to say any of them.

"Have you started your Christmas shopping?" the woman asked.

Joseph squinted at her, then quickly relaxed his face to not look as though she'd asked a ridiculous question. But for crying out loud, it was the first week of November. "No," he said.

She nodded.

He scanned the nearest shelf. Maybe he could buy a little trinket so as not to completely waste her time. There was a ceramic kitten with big eyes. Joseph's mom liked cats. And she was the only person on his Christmas list, the one he couldn't believe this woman had him considering so insanely early. He picked up the kitten and checked the price. Then he put it back down as slowly and carefully as he could. He was not about to drop that kind of cash on a paperweight.

"I'll look over here," he said. He moved to another shelf, trying to pretend he might find something more appropriate over there. He was wasting her time now for sure.

A pair of sharp eyes followed him.

His own eyes traveled over many more knickknacks without really seeing them until he felt he'd stalled long enough. He took a step towards the door and turned back, "Have a nice day."

There was no one there to acknowledge his words. The old woman must have moved behind a shelf. He didn't look for her. He pushed open the door and walked outside. No sign of Jillian.

Joseph hurried down Main Street. He paused in front of the glass door to Mr. Sweet's insurance agency to wave at his sister. She was on the phone with her head bent over her desk. Ella saw him though. She waved, which made Ruth look up and stick her tongue out at her brother.

He resisted the urge to make a face back. Ruth was twenty-three, and he was six years older. He and his siblings seemed to revert to their younger selves when they were together. Or in sight of each other.

There wasn't much else of interest between the insurance place and his destination, Seymour's Grocery. The automatic doors slid open, and he stepped into the brightly lit store. Before his eyes fully adjusted, he heard someone call out his name. "Joseph Ziebert! Just the person I was hoping to see."

He stopped and prepared to fight a losing battle. "Hello, Mrs. Donnelly."

She had gray streaks in her dark hair and a bulging plastic bag hanging from each hand. "How are you today?" she asked pleasantly.

He wasn't fooled by the small talk. She was about to get him to volunteer for something. He'd say she was going to *try* to get him to volunteer for something, but no one said no to Mrs. Donnelly. "Fine, thanks," he said. "How about you?"

"Oh, it's a lovely day," she said. Her smile faded as she tipped her head forward so that her eyes stared seriously at him over the tops of her glasses. "You know St. Jude's Fall Festival is coming up, right?"

Joseph nodded. Then he actually thought about it and realized how close it was. "I believe it's next Sunday." He'd just gotten his work schedule and knew he'd be off that Sunday. He would have no legitimate excuse for whatever she was about to ask.

"That's right," she said. She took a step to the side to clear a path for other shoppers. "One thing we still need is someone to emcee the cake walk." Her eyes darted away from his only a moment to give the impression she was about to share a secret. "Right now,

I'm looking at a young man with a deep, commanding voice that I know would be perfect for the job. People will love to hear you call their numbers, don't you think?"

"Well, I suppose…" If he called someone's number, it would mean he or she had just won a cake. It was difficult to argue that anyone wouldn't be happy about that, given the purpose of entering.

"Do you know how the cake walk works?" she asked.

He nodded. It was pretty simple. He'd even won himself a cake a few years earlier.

"You don't have to work that Sunday?"

"No, I don't," he admitted.

"And you didn't already tell someone else you'd work a different booth?"

"No," he said slowly, because now he felt guilty about that and no one had even asked him.

"Great." She smiled broadly. "I can tell the pastor you'll be our emcee?"

Joseph nodded, trying not to look reluctant. He'd probably go to the festival anyway, and the cake walk would only take an hour or so.

"It's at 2 o'clock, but you'll need to be there about a half hour early to set up," she said.

The emcee also had to set up?

"And we only need six more cakes. You can get anyone you like to help you bake those. See you next Sunday."

She smiled so brightly as she left that he instinctively returned it. It helped that he was completely in awe of the woman's recruiting skills. He'd just volunteered to bake six cakes, and he didn't own an oven. Mrs. Donnelly was good.

Joseph turned and picked up a shopping basket. Should he call his mom right away to ask if she'd bake some cakes or wait until he saw her in person? He decided that in person would be better mostly because it would be later. He tossed a few veggies and a loaf of bread into his basket before heading to the lunch meat section.

He recognized the woman standing in front of the case. She had layered brown hair and wore a gray sweater with sequins woven into it. Joseph had met her only once before at a young adult meeting a few weeks earlier. Her name was Emily. She had the same big red bag slung over her shoulder now as when they met. At first, he thought she was being indecisive, but then he realized she was distracted by the phone pressed to her ear.

There was a package of roast beef he could grab without getting in her way. He was about to reach for it when she picked up some meat near it and tossed it onto the floor. She'd clearly meant to drop it in her basket.

Joseph picked it up. It was turkey. He intended to set it in her basket for her. But she was already walking away, apparently unaware that she'd missed her target. He waved the package in the air, thinking maybe he could get her attention without interrupting the phone call. When that didn't work, he wasn't sure what to do. She hadn't paid for the turkey yet. He could just put it back in the case. What if she got all the way home before she realized she didn't have it and had to make a second trip? Andauk was a tiny town so it wouldn't be a long trip. Joseph would still be annoyed if it happened to him. He began to follow Emily. He tried to stay back far enough so as not to overhear any of her conversation but close enough that he'd be able to tell when she hung up.

****

Emily Mayor was staring at cans. There were a ton of options on the shelves in front of her. All the colorful labels blended together. She knew she'd come into this aisle for something, but it was hard to concentrate with her dad yammering in her ear.

"I saw two newborns this week," he said.

"Mm-hmm."

"I know you miss the tiny babies."

"Of course I do."

"Your mom wants me to ask if you're still on a diet."

"I'm not calling it a diet," Emily said. "But I'm still hoping to lose ten more pounds." She'd put on twenty pounds in the two years after college. She lost five pounds the first week after deciding to eat better. The next five took a month.

"You know you're beautiful, right?"

She rolled her eyes. "Yes, Dad. But you're a doctor. I would think you'd want me to take care of myself."

"Of course I do. But your mom worries about you having body image issues."

"I know she does. I'm not starving myself. I've read all the charts in your office. My target weight is a healthy weight and where I was for years. Also, we've had this conversation at least five times already."

"Thanks for humoring me a sixth time," he said. "You're not eating that sugar-free garbage, are you?"

"No, Dad." An involuntary smile popped up at the hint of a very familiar lecture. Her dad was strongly opposed to artificial sweeteners. It had more to do with his taste buds than his medical license. "I'm just trying to eat more fruits and vegetables and less dessert. So far it's working. I like peas and oh, that fruit cocktail with the extra cherries." She said out loud what she put into her basket to help her concentrate.

"And have you met any nice young men in your area?"

"There are plenty of nice people here." She knew what he

meant but hoped he'd take the hint that she hadn't met anyone worth mentioning.

He heard the hint. Emily knew he heard it. "Well, if you want to bring me some little patients someday," he said, "you need to start dating one of those nice people."

"Not that easy, Dad."

"Sure it is. You don't need to wait around for heart flutters or some meet cute," he said. "Just sign up for one of those dating sites and filter through the guys like job applicants. You know what you want."

Emily sighed. Her dad was not exactly a hopeless romantic. She wasn't about to tell him she'd tried his advice. She found a couple of guys with potential. Both of them lived hundreds of miles away, which might have been more disappointing than meeting someone local with less potential. "Well... I'll keep that in mind," she said dismissively.

A doubtful grunt came through the phone. "You know, your mom met a young man she thinks you might like, but he hasn't been properly vetted yet."

Properly vetted? Emily could just imagine going out with a guy after he'd been hand-picked by her mom. She was trying to be the one running her own show. It was time to change the subject. "What kind of cereal do you like, Dad?" She'd apparently wandered into the cereal aisle.

He laughed. "All right, honey. I'll let you get back to your shopping."

"Thanks. Talk to you later." She put the phone in her bag and really looked at the cereal. Did she need cereal? She took a box off the shelf and spoke to the cartoon character on the front. "I'm not going to buy you because marshmallows don't fit into my healthier eating plan. But maybe you can tell me why every conversation with my dad sounds like the last conversation with my dad."

"Emily?"

She jumped so bad she almost dropped the box.

"Sorry. I didn't mean to scare you."

Emily's mind raced to process the situation. The only other person in the aisle was a guy with curly black hair, fair but slightly freckled skin and a powerful-looking build. Her first thought was that this was someone who took care of himself. The second was that he seemed vaguely familiar and knew her name. That meant they must have met at some point, though she couldn't remember when or where. The last thought – and it was the one that kept her mouth hanging open with no words coming out – was that this very handsome man was standing there watching her talk to a box of cereal.

"I, uh…" He glanced down uncertainly and held out a package of some sort of lunch meat. "Did you want this?"

Did she want a random package of meat? Perhaps this guy was as crazy as she was. Unless that was a terrible pickup line? She would be fully prepared to forgive that.

"Because you dropped it," he added.

"I did?" Was that turkey? She'd been planning to buy turkey but didn't remember getting it yet. She pushed the cereal onto the shelf and let go too quickly. It pitched forward and bounced off her shoulder on the way to the floor. For goodness' sake! Six years of ballet. Two years of gymnastics. Three of karate, three of soccer. And still Emily was about as graceful as a stampeding buffalo.

She picked up the box and replaced it more carefully. Then she held out her hand for the turkey so this guy would go away and let her die of embarrassment in peace. "Thank you," she mumbled.

He did not go away. "It is Emily, right?"

"Yes. Have we met?" She had no dignity left. She might as well admit she had no memory either.

"At St. Jude's. The Friday night young adult group?" He widened his eyes, hoping for some recognition to dawn.

She'd been to two of those meetings, three if you counted the one when she'd shown up as everyone else was leaving and oh, gosh. That was why he looked familiar. He'd been there when she'd foolishly gotten the time wrong. She remembered that he'd introduced himself, but what was his name? She shook her head pathetically.

"Joseph Ziebert." He smiled and held out his hand.

"Emily Mayor," she said, though he probably already knew that. By some miracle, she managed to shake his hand without dropping anything else. His grip was strong and the way its warmth lingered on her skin added to her flustered desire to escape.

"Have you been back?" Joseph asked. He didn't seem nearly as anxious to run away.

"Uh, what?" she said.

"Have you been back?"

Emily looked over her shoulder. "I mean, back where?"

"The young adult group," he said. "My work schedule doesn't let me go every week… at least right now. I wondered if I missed you the last few weeks."

"Oh. Right. Yes, I was there on time the last couple." *Way to remind him how you got it wrong the first time.*

"What do you think?"

"Of?" This might be the most incoherent conversation of her life.

He smiled, possibly trying not to laugh at her outright. "The meetings. Do you like it so far?"

"Uh, I guess. The leaders don't do much. She just reads some questions from a book and then we all talk."

"That's my sister," he said with a nod.

His sister? Did she just insult his sister? Things were going from worse to really really worse every time Emily opened her mouth.

"Are you going tonight?"

"Um…" She was. She'd been intending to go but now she was afraid Joseph would be there, and she wouldn't be able to show her face. "Are you going?" She did not just ask him that.

He nodded and gestured to his shopping basket. "Just needed to get some dinner first."

Well, now she couldn't say she was skipping because he might think it had something to do with him when it would have everything to do with him and the way she was thoroughly humiliating herself in front of him. She pointed to her own basket. "Sounds like we have the same plan," she said.

"Okay." He smiled again. It was a nice smile, like donating a million dollars was nice. "I should let you finish then. See you later."

Emily gave a quick wave, then turned back to the cereal determined not to let him catch her watching him walk away. She managed to salvage that crumb. The smiling character on the box now seemed to be laughing at her.

"You saw that whole thing, didn't you?" she said. "Man, he was cute though. He mentioned a work schedule and going to my church and family and… If this worked my dad's way, I could be checking off so many boxes. Instead, it works the real way where I dig myself a hole and stick my foot in the hole and my mouth and…" Emily stopped and shook her head at the metaphor she was killing.

A hand reached for a box near her. There was a woman standing right behind her who smiled politely as she took the box away. Great. Another person had caught her talking to cereal. Where were all the squeaky-wheeled carts when she needed them?

2

Emily stood in her closet facing a huge decision. Actually, she stood in her closet working a teeny tiny decision into something huge. Should she change her clothes or not? She was still wearing the sweater and dress pants she'd worn to work. She wanted to put on something more comfortable before going to the church group. But Joseph would be there.

She wanted to look as nice as possible because she had a lot of ground to cover to make up for the awful impression she'd made at the store. She kind of wanted to put on that navy dress. It had a flattering cut with pretty material that was really comfortable. She'd gotten plenty of compliments in that.

But it was a dress. Joseph had already seen her wearing this outfit. If she changed into a dress, it'd be obvious she was trying to impress someone. Would he think it was weird if she changed? Would he think she appreciated the chance to be more casual? Or would he think she didn't care about the group because she'd already accused his sister of being lazy? Was there any chance at all that he even noticed what she was wearing while she was dropping stuff at his feet?

Emily grabbed a pair of jeans and switched her heels for sneakers. She wasn't going to meet guys anyway. Not exactly. She hoped to make some friends, and if one of them happened to be a guy that would be awesome. It would just have to be a guy who liked her in jeans. And probably not the one who thought she was a lunatic anyway.

The parking lot behind the church was pretty empty when Emily shut off her car. There were four other cars, at least one that she recognized from other Fridays. There was an elementary school attached to the church. That was where the meetings were held. She walked quickly towards the door as the temperature felt very much like a November evening in Ohio.

The hallway was already familiar. So far, Emily liked St. Jude's better than her old parish. That was not to say she had anything against the old one. She was just happy that *something* about her move had gone right.

She'd moved to Andauk about six weeks ago to escape her parents, which wasn't as bad as it sounded either. She wasn't trying to avoid them, and they hadn't been fighting. But up until six weeks ago, Emily had been a twenty-six-year-old woman living with her parents who worked for her parents and drove between the two in the car her parents gave her. When her mom had started suggesting she could help her find a husband, Emily knew it was time to do something. She was trying to unspoil herself. She kept the car though. The goal was unspoiled, not impoverished.

Voices spilled out of the meeting room and several of them greeted Emily as she entered. It was a friendly group. She didn't want to think of it as a place to meet a man, but the thought tugged at the back of her mind as she took a seat across from two happy couples.

Isaac and Jessica were married and expecting their first child before Christmas. Last week the baby had been kicking so strongly they could all see Jessica's tummy jump. Gabriel and Ruth, the group's leaders, were dating. It seemed this was a recent development by the teasing from some of the others. Ella was the only other person in the circle so far. Her hair was braided over her shoulder, and she looked different without glasses.

"You look nice today," Emily said to her. "Do you wear contacts often?"

Ella sort of shook her head and shrugged at the same time.

Emily worked to dislodge her foot. "I'm not suggesting you should," she corrected. "You look good in glasses, too. I mostly meant your hair looks nice. Not that it doesn't usually."

"Thank you," Ella said. Her smile said she had taken no offense at the inept compliment. Or the babbling that followed it.

"Hi, everyone." A dark-haired man came in with a wave for the group. Emily thought she detected some Hispanic heritage but could be wrong. Maybe Native American? Maybe he worked outside and kept a tan all year.

She said hello with the others. His name was Sebastian, and she'd met him at the last meeting. He was a nice-looking man, particularly his eyes. There was something confident yet hesitant about the way he looked at everyone. It was difficult to describe other than to say it was highly appealing. Unfortunately, Emily had picked up a vibe that suggested those eyes were interested in Ella. It was possible she was wrong. She was wrong a lot. It felt safer not to set her sights on him though, just in case.

Her sights landed on the next person to enter the room. Joseph. He saw her, too. His eyes landed on each of them in turn, but there was a moment of either happiness or amusement when he looked at Emily. The knowledge that it was more likely the latter made her own gaze dive to the floor in embarrassment.

She was still completely aware of him claiming the chair next to hers. It meant nothing. There were not a lot of other empty chairs, and he immediately began chatting with Isaac. Then Julia entered. Emily had talked to her briefly before each of the meetings so far.

Julia was also somewhat new in town. She smiled when she saw Emily. They exchanged pleasantries as several side conversations went on around them until it was time to begin.

Gabriel led them in an opening prayer. She wondered if he had to come straight from work since he always wore a tie. Another guy came in after the amen, apologizing for being late. He looked like Gabriel. Unless she was imagining things, there was a strong family resemblance between the two of them.

"Hey, Eric," Isaac said.

"Glad you *finally* made it," Gabriel said.

Eric nodded at everyone as he took the last seat. He smiled at Emily and Julia, though it seemed mostly for Julia.

"Today we're going to talk about St. John Vianney." Gabriel looked at the notebook in his lap and read a brief biography. "He's the patron saint of priests. It's said that he sometimes heard confessions for sixteen hours a day."

"Hey, that reminds me of our first question," Ruth said.

Gabriel grinned at what was clearly a planned interruption.

"Can any of you think of something you'd be willing to do for sixteen hours a day?"

"Sleep," Jessica said, rubbing a hand on her belly. "Or at least try to."

There were a few sympathetic chuckles. People started to look around the room to see if anyone else had anything to say.

"Sixteen hours *every* day?" Joseph asked.

Ruth shrugged at him. "At least occasionally."

He shook his head. "That doesn't leave time for much else."

"Yeah, that's dedication," Sebastian said.

"I can't imagine anything that anyone would want me to do for sixteen hours," Eric said. "And I think that would sort of be the point of..." He trailed off as he couldn't find the right words to finish.

Nods around the room meant most people understood his basic point.

Emily stayed quiet. She didn't have an answer either.

When it seemed the question had run its course, Ruth tried another one. "So he's the priest of... I mean, the patron of priests and vocations. This tripped me up because I didn't realize that vocation could mean... I thought it strictly referred to joining a religious order, but it just means following God's plan for your life. The question we –"

Joseph interrupted her with an impatient sound. "You didn't know that?" he asked with disbelief.

"No."

"How many years have I been talking about finding my vocation?"

Ruth fidgeted in her chair. "I thought you meant it as a... a kind of joke. Since you decided *not* to go to seminary."

Emily felt her head whip towards the man next to her. Joseph had considered becoming a priest? Why did that information grab her attention? People did have a natural inclination to want things they couldn't have. But he'd apparently decided against those vows. There shouldn't be anything in a rejected path to suddenly make him more attractive. Emily brushed all those thoughts from her head. She never should have taken that psychology class.

"So anyway," Ruth continued, "while Joseph is still figuring out his vocation, is anyone doing something that you think of as, well, as something God has called you to do?"

"I might be working on mine," Joseph said. He smiled mysteriously.

"Really?" Isaac looked intrigued.

"But I'm not ready to talk about it," Joseph added. "Except... Sebastian, can I talk to you for a minute when we're done here?"

Sebastian looked surprised, but he nodded.

"Great."

"I wonder if leading this group was God's plan for me or just Mrs. Donnelly's plan for me."

A few people laughed at Gabriel's remark. Ruth gave him a rather sappy look. The group had evidently brought the two of them together so Emily knew what was behind that expression. But then Ruth looked right at her and said, "What about you, Emily?"

"Uh... what about me?"

"I don't mean to put you on the spot," Ruth said. "It's just that I feel like we know very little about you. What do you do for a living?"

"Right now I work in a dentist's office in Pinebury."

Isaac smiled kindly. "You don't say that like it's a calling or even something you want to keep doing."

"No." Emily shook her head. "I want to quit, but I need to find a new job first."

"What do you want to do?" Sebastian asked.

"Or how did you end up there?" Isaac looked as though he was trying to remember something. "Because I think you said you got a new job when you moved here, and that wasn't very long ago."

"Well, I guess I could start at the beginning." Emily glanced around to see if the others looked interested. Her past would be easier to relate because her future was so uncertain. All eyes were on her so she started talking. "My dad is a doctor, a pediatrician. My mom is a nurse. They work together in the same office. There are a couple other doctors there. Anyway, as long as I can remember my dad was talking about me being a doctor just like him. My mom encouraged it, too. I was excited about it because I pretty much thought he spent his days playing with babies. I love babies. Then when I got to high school, I began to understand a lot better what the job of pediatrician entails. It's not a job for me."

She shrugged apologetically as a reflex, even though her parents weren't around. "All those years of school. And some kids have serious illnesses and... I don't think my heart could take that. It's just not a job for me. But I felt like I'd sort of led my parents on that that's what I was going to do for so long that I wasn't clear or forceful enough when I realized I didn't want it. I think I acted more indecisive than I was. They ended up suggesting I put off college for a year while I thought about it. I worked at a fast food place most of that time, which ended up being two years.

"My parents accepted that I wasn't going to be a doctor, but they were pushing me to get an MBA and come work for them and eventually run their office, which I have to admit was partially because I wasn't figuring out any direction of my own. I started a business degree but kept waffling about what I wanted to do and ended up finishing just a four-year degree.

"I still went to work with my parents. I was mostly handling insurance paperwork. It wasn't a terrible job but, well... I guess I just wanted to pick something for myself. I moved out of my parents' house – yes, just last month at twenty-six – as soon as I got the receptionist gig at the dentist office. I moved to Andauk to... I hate to say find myself. Maybe we can say I'm finding my vocation. But it's not going well at all. Everything keeps breaking in my apartment. I've had to call the landlord like four or five times.

"The job is all kinds of awful. I spend a lot of time on the phone making or changing appointments and there are three dentists and most of the patients request a specific one but they're all in the same spreadsheet in the worst format ever. It's impossible to read and so embarrassing to be on the phone with someone who's asking if I found 1 o'clock yet without being able to explain that the system is broken. Meanwhile, two of the hygienists are always on each other's case about taking someone's supplies or moving them or not ordering enough or… It's just constant bickering."

Emily sighed as she finished and cringed at the same time. She was completely monopolizing the meeting. She tentatively peeked around the room and was relieved to see that no one was glaring or rolling their eyes at her rant. They actually seemed pleased to know more about her.

Then Joseph said, "Eleven years."

"Is that how long I've been talking?"

He let out a short, surprised laugh.

He had not been trying to joke about her lengthy speech, which made Emily feel stupid for pointing it out.

"No," he said. "If we both started hunting a vocation at eighteen, I've been at it for eleven years to your eight. You have three more years until it counts as a long time or else I'm just failing."

"Except that I haven't been looking for most of those eight years," Emily said. "It's more like I was delaying looking."

Sebastian raised a hand. "Yeah, if we get to count from eighteen, I'd be up to ten years. But I'm with Emily in that I spent a lot of that time sort of… drifting. I've only been trying to find some purpose the last year or two."

Emily watched his eyes sweep the room as he talked and noticed how they stuttered at Ella. She wasn't wrong. There was a clear desire to include Ella in the purpose.

"So you guys are saying I'm the only one who's trying and failing?" Joseph said darkly. "Thanks."

"I don't think anyone who is trying is failing, at least not in God's eyes," Jessica said.

"Oh." A smile twitched while Sebastian tried to look offended. "So it's us drifters who are failures?"

"I didn't say that," Jessica said. "I'm only saying that we don't all necessarily have one vocation our entire lives. Maybe the drifters and searchers were working on another vocation, maybe one you didn't even recognize, and now you're ready for something new. A year ago, I might have said that teaching was my vocation. Now I'm not sure I want to go back to it after the baby." She rubbed a hand over her belly. "This might be my new vocation."

"Or maybe the drifting has somehow prepared you for what's coming," Isaac suggested.

"And the searching?" Joseph sounded skeptical. "That's preparation?"

"Until you know what you want to do," Isaac said, "you don't know how you need to prepare for it."

Several people chuckled at the defensive tone. Emily didn't laugh. There was surprisingly profound truth in his flippant statement, and it gave her comfort. If God could make beauty from ashes, he could use what she thought of as wasting her life for some future good.

They talked for a few minutes about the fact that a life's purpose didn't need to be anything grand. The next question related to how to know when you were following God's plan for you. That one was discussed with a lot of shrugs and a few smiles. The time for the meeting passed quickly.

"Before we wrap up," Gabriel said with a glance at the clock, "Mrs. Donnelly wanted me to remind everyone about the Fall Festival next Sunday. She wants us to come and spend money to support the church. Also, it might not be a bad place to find some new members for our group. So put it on your calendars."

"And it can be kind of fun," Ruth added.

"Wait! Speaking of the festival…" Joseph paused to get everyone's attention. A couple of people had pulled out phones, presumably to check or add something to their calendars. "Mrs.

Donnelly cornered me at Seymour's earlier today."

Isaac started laughing. "And what are you in charge of now?"

"The cake walk," Joseph answered with an overly dramatic sigh.

"That doesn't last all day," Sebastian said. "It shouldn't be too bad."

"That's what I thought and why I agreed. However…" He closed his eyes and looked almost like a man about to announce a death sentence. "As soon as I agreed, she said, 'And by the way, we need six more cakes.' So now I think I need six more cakes." He opened his eyes again and looked around hopefully. Then he tacked on an ingratiating smile.

Emily had to turn away to settle the crazy flip flops in her stomach.

"I'll make you a cake," Jessica said.

"Awesome. You are now my favorite sister-in-law."

Jessica was Joseph's sister-in-law? That meant he and Isaac were brothers, something Emily did not know.

"I can make one, too," Gabriel said.

Ruth turned to him. "Do you have some kind of old-fashioned cake pan?"

"No," he said. "Oh! But I would love to try to make frosting with a butter churn."

"You have a butter churn?" Emily asked.

When he nodded, she shared a bemused expression with Julia. None of the others seemed remotely surprised that the guy owned a butter churn. It was yet another reminder of how much of an outsider she was. Perhaps this was a chance for Emily to join in.

"I might be able to make a cake," she said to Joseph. "It doesn't have to be anything fancy, does it?"

He shook his head. "It just has to look good enough to eat."

"Okay. I can do that." She really hoped she could do that. But nothing had been going right lately so she had some doubts. "Should I just bring it on the day of the festival?"

"Yeah. It starts at two. I'm supposed to be there by 1:30. Do you think you could bring it during that window?" Joseph had turned his entire body to face her, and the others were beginning to stand up and put their chairs away.

Emily began to feel as though the two of them were having a private conversation. Her imagination and his deep brown eyes made her get all mushy as though he was asking her on a date and not simply arranging to be handed a cake. "Okay," she said, then swallowed to keep her voice from cracking again. "1:30 with a cake. It's in the gym?"

"The cake walk will be." He flashed a smile. "That's where you'll find me. But there will be other events all over the parking lot and in a few of the classrooms."

She nodded.

He stood up to help rearrange the room.

Emily tried to get out of the way. The handle on her bag got hooked on her chair. She dragged the legs across the floor for two screechy seconds before she untangled herself and made a hasty exit.

3

Joseph pulled the collar of his robe a little tighter. He kept his heat low to save money. It only bothered him first thing in the morning. His internal heat didn't seem to wake up the same time as the rest of him. After breakfast, he would take a nice hot shower and be fine the rest of the day. The milk on his cereal felt extra cold that morning. At least he hoped that was the cause of the shiver, and not a sense of foreboding.

He didn't know how his family would react to the news he planned to share that day. He'd been working on this dream for so long he was both thrilled and terrified that it was on the verge of happening. His parents' reaction could make him more thrilled or more terrified. And he just knew his mom would want a tour.

She was going to hate this apartment. She was going to hate that he hadn't bothered to paint over the plaster where the walls had been opened to fix the wiring. She was going to hate that he was feeding himself with a mini fridge and a microwave. She was going to hate the hole in the door to the bedroom and how cold it was.

As far as Joseph was concerned though, the place was livable. It didn't have to be pretty. It was upstairs, and upstairs didn't matter. He spent most of his time on the first floor and planned to continue once it was open. In fact, he was going to try out the mats that had finally arrived after church and before lunch at his parents' house.

He went to the earlier Mass because he had to get up so early

– usually by 3 AM on the days he worked – and didn't want to swing the pendulum too far on the other days. Of course, that work schedule would only be for two more weeks. He'd still get up early when he was his own boss, but at an hour he chose.

He'd worked up quite an appetite by the time the others would be finishing church. And a need for another shower. The workout still hadn't settled his nerves.

Either they had a short homily or Joseph had been dragging his feet more than he realized because he appeared to be the last to arrive. There was a line of cars along the street next to his parents' house. First was his mom's car, then his dad's. Ruth was parked behind him. Gabriel usually walked to church and probably got a ride with Ruth. Then was Isaac's car, who would of course have Jessica with him. And the last car was Ella's.

Joseph was afraid there might be a problem brewing there. Ella had only been joining the family for Sunday lunch as long as Gabriel, about a month. She was Ruth's friend and Isaac had invited both of them to help plan the saints they would talk about on Fridays. But as far as Joseph knew – he'd missed a couple of Sundays for work so he could be wrong – they'd never done any planning over lunch. That and the way everyone else was paired up made him suspect people had matchmaking plans.

He was not interested in dating Ella. He'd already considered the possibility. There weren't a lot of options in a small town, and he definitely wanted to get married so he considered most of the women he came across. While Ella was pretty and from what he could tell seemed nice, he just wasn't drawn to her the way he felt drawn to someone else. Which was a problem for a different day.

If Ella was not one of the people with matchmaking plans, the two of them could simply laugh at his family's efforts. If she did have any designs on him, he might eventually end up hurting her feelings.

That was certainly an idea that made him cringe. But it was something else he didn't plan to worry about that particular Sunday. There were bigger fish to fry.

Fish was not literally on the menu. Joseph smelled pizza as soon as he walked in the back door. Then he was ambushed.

"There you are!"

"Did you forget how to tell time?"

"The pizza is getting cold, man."

"Have you checked your phone?"

"Sorry I'm late," Joseph said, pulling out his phone. He'd been texted by three family members in the last ten minutes. "Guess you guys are hungry."

"We were smelling it even when it was still in the oven," Ruth said.

Isaac turned away from Joseph to their mom. "Can we eat now?"

She nodded and instructed them to form a line by the stack of plates.

Joseph was behind his sister. "I assume we're not expecting Adam," he whispered.

"No," she said simply.

It wasn't surprising, but it was unfortunate. Adam was his other brother. He was older than Ruth and younger than Joseph. He'd been avoiding family gatherings more and more since he had been with Kayla. The family tried not to act as though they disapproved, but the woman made it difficult by being negative about everything. Things had gotten a lot worse after Adam announced their engagement. Kayla had tried to joke about how they didn't have to worry because she'd be an excellent first wife.

All eight of them fit around the dining room table. Joseph ended up sitting between Isaac and Gabriel with Ella directly across from him. She only ended up there because Ruth and Jessica had taken places across from their significant others. Still, it emphasized the pairings in the room. Joseph blocked out the seating arrangement while they blessed the food. He needed to concentrate on his announcement.

He never got to say the words that he'd rehearsed though. He was about to find out that he'd waited just a little too long to share the news.

His mother began the conversation almost in the same breath as her amen. "Joseph," she said sternly, "we need to talk."

It sounded as though she was about to yell at him for not cleaning his room. He instinctively tried to look innocent.

"I had a rather disturbing chat with Travis Shannon yesterday," she said.

Mr. Shannon was a former neighbor and the real estate agent who'd sold Joseph his building. What were the odds this disturbing news had nothing to do with the man's job? Joseph figured they were not good. He braced himself.

"I bumped into him at Seymour's," his mom explained. "He asked me when you planned to open. I said, 'Open what?' and he said, 'It's been almost a year since he bought the old apothecary. I guessed he'd be getting close to opening by now.'" She raised her eyebrows deliberately to indicate her shock.

"What?" Ruth said.

"You bought the old apothecary?" Isaac asked.

There was plenty of surprise to go around. Joseph's dad was the only one who didn't look shocked. He'd likely already heard about it when his parents hashed out exactly how to grill him about it.

"Yes," was all Joseph said because his mom was very upset. It didn't feel like the right moment to get her excited about his plans.

"When?" she asked. "Has it really been almost a year?"

"I closed in January."

"January? And when were you going to tell us about this?"

He sighed. She wasn't going to believe him, but he admitted he'd been about to bring it up.

"That's convenient," she said.

"Wait." Isaac put down his slice of pizza as a thought occurred to him. "That old building has an apartment upstairs. Are you living there?"

Joseph winced as he nodded. This was not at all how he imagined the lunch.

His mom's eyes got bigger than the pizza as everyone else joined in his wince.

"Joseph," she said. She wasn't shouting. Her voice was eerily calm and quiet. "Am I hearing correctly? Did you *move* and not tell anyone?"

"I, uh… did."

"Have you been living there since January?" Ruth asked.

He shook his head. "It took a while to get ready since I did a lot of the work myself. I moved in April."

"April?" His mom's eyes were still bugging out. "For more than six months I haven't known where my own child lives?"

"Well, I always come here," Joseph said, "so it hasn't really come up."

"What if there was some kind of emergency, and I needed to get in touch with you?"

He pulled his phone out of his pocket and waved it at her. "You haven't had any trouble getting in touch with me."

"I don't know," Ruth said. "You haven't replied to the text I sent you a half hour ago."

Before he put the phone away, Joseph typed out: I'll be there twenty minutes ago.

Ruth laughed when she saw it and held it across the table for Gabriel to read. Their dad cleared his throat then, and she quickly put the phone away. They weren't supposed to have them in sight during meals and there were already enough strained nerves.

"I believe we've given Joseph enough of a hard time about what he hasn't told us," their dad said. He had red hair like Isaac and Adam and Ruth and his wife. Joseph rarely felt like an oddball for being the only dark-haired family member. But in that moment, he felt like an outsider for entirely different reasons. "What are your plans? I've seen the paper on the windows for a long time so I've known someone had plans for the building. I'll be glad to hear them."

Joseph nodded. He turned to the other end of the table to look at his mom.

She gave him one last stern look followed by a slow blink. Then just like that she looked ready to listen and hear him out.

"I plan to open a gym."

There was a lot of slow nodding as they all waited to hear more.

"It's not a traditional gym but a place where families can come and be active together. I'm not putting in any big expensive equipment. There's a track around the outside for walking or jogging and I have medicine balls and jump ropes and hula hoops and… there will be some free play times but mostly I want to have a lot of different classes."

"Martial arts?" Isaac asked.

"Some," Joseph said with a nod. "Master Bob agreed to teach a class or two with me." Joseph had taken karate for a year before switching to hapkido long enough to earn a black belt. Master Bob had been his instructor for the latter. "You know he retired a while back. I think he's bored now because he was excited about coming back to teach just a few hours a week. So excited he doesn't want to be paid."

"A few hours a week?" Jessica's ears had perked up. "Were you thinking of doing a mommy and baby class?"

"Is that idea more or less attractive if we pretend I hadn't already thought about asking you to lead one?"

She laughed and more importantly appeared fully on board without him actually having to ask.

"I like the idea," Ruth said. "I'm not teaching any classes, but I like the idea."

"Thank you," Joseph said. "And I already thought about *not* asking you."

His dad was nodding his approval as well. "When do you expect to open?"

"I'm looking at January," Joseph said. "You know there will be lots of people making resolutions to be more active and spend more time with their kids. This is both."

"Good thinking," Isaac said.

"I'm getting ready to kick up some advertising. Mrs. Wellington thinks it's a great idea." Mrs. Wellington was the principal at the elementary school where both Joseph's mom and sister-in-law worked. They nodded at his mention of her name. "She's willing to pass out flyers with an interest survey to help me figure out which classes might be popular and what times. We'll distribute those as soon as I get everything working on the website. Sebastian Jones agreed to help me with some technical issues. Said he'd have time tomorrow night."

Joseph's mom dropped her pizza crust onto her plate and began to count on her fingers. "Marie Wellington, Sebastian Jones, Master Bob, Travis Shannon. I'm hearing a whole list of people who knew about your plans before your mother."

"I haven't needed your help with anything yet."

"So you only talk to your mother when you need something?"

There was a note in her voice that warned of the consequences of agreeing.

He was there every Sunday he could so they both knew it wasn't true. All the same, he made a mental note to put off asking her about those three cakes he still needed.

Joseph's dad was chewing thoughtfully, both on the pizza and the new information. He appeared much more willing to overlook the delay in sharing. "You plan to recruit from the middle school as well?"

"I hope so," Joseph said. "I've called the principal there three times, and he still hasn't called me back."

"I'm thinking you can't do all this and drive a truck," Ruth said with a leading tone.

"Nope. I already put in my notice."

"Really?" Ruth looked surprised. She also looked impressed, which lifted Joseph's spirits. He'd expected the loss of his job to be the hardest part for everyone to swallow. Perhaps it was the part that let them believe he was serious. "That means since I don't have to work next Sunday, I can start being here every week."

"Every week?" Isaac asked. "You're not going to be open on Sundays?"

"No. Besides wanting to keep Sunday apart, I expect Saturday to be my longest and busiest day so I'll need the rest."

"A silver lining." His mom gave him a genuine smile. For all the fuss, she wasn't really angry with him. She was just feeling left out. "We're going to start getting updates on this venture every Sunday from now on?"

"Yes. For what it's worth, I'm sorry you found out from someone else. I wanted to have a good plan so I could surprise you."

"You're forgiven," she said. "But I want a tour, like yesterday."

****

Joseph walked into the dispatch office a few days later to pick up his last week's schedule. Then he walked out again. Jillian was in there alone, and thank heavens she hadn't seen him. He took his phone from his pocket and tried to decide how to waste a few minutes. Maybe he could text his mom about those cakes now.

Joseph: Mrs. Donnelly wants three more cakes for the walk. Can you help me with them?

She replied right away. Mom: Do you want me to help or do you want me to do it for you?

He didn't know if he'd actually been vague or if she was reading it that way on purpose because she wasn't quite over the secrecy. He'd probably get back in her good graces in a hurry if he offered to do it together. Joseph: Are you free Saturday afternoon? I can come over after work.

Mom: Or I could come see your new place.

Drat. He needed to get her in a good mood before she saw his modest quarters.

Joseph: I don't have all the necessary supplies.

"Like an oven," he mumbled to himself.

Mom: All right. Saturday it is. See you soon. :)

"Hey, man, hear you're on your way out." The welcome voice of a coworker arriving on the scene.

"Yeah," Joseph said. "I'm about to grab my last schedule."

"Hope Mr. D. is in," the other guy said as he opened the door.

Joseph nodded. He could still hope for that even if Joseph already knew it wasn't true. He sensed the other guy's steps slow as his hopes were dashed.

"Hello, boys." Jillian stood from her desk and walked around to sit on the front of it. "Here for your schedules?"

"Of course," other guy said.

Joseph would be trying harder to remember his name if it wasn't likely the last time he'd ever see him.

"What's the magic word?" Jillian asked. She began to twirl a chunk of bright red hair around her finger. It wasn't red like the Ziebert redheads but like someone dumped a can of paint on her head.

"Now," other guy said. He sounded even less in the mood to play games than Joseph.

Jillian had been testing everyone's patience, and she'd only worked there for three months. She was somewhere in her forties but acted like a child, though she certainly didn't dress like one. Even now that it felt like winter and the rest of her was covered, she insisted on wearing a neckline that didn't come anywhere near her neck.

She pouted at the impatient response. "You boys never want to stay and chat with me."

"Sorry, Jillian," Joseph said. "It's been a long day." That was true even if he couldn't say he'd be more inclined to stick around at the beginning of a shift.

Jillian leaned forward. "Do you want to get together some time when you're less tired?"

Joseph took a small step backwards while the other guy said, "Just hand over the schedules."

"Fine." She was still pouting, but she went back around her desk and picked up a folder. She apparently found Joseph's first because she held out a slip of paper to him. He was seriously relieved because he was afraid if the other guy got his schedule first, he'd take off and leave Joseph alone with Jillian. She'd asked him out at least ten times already. He'd already stopped trying to be polite about it, but he was afraid if he made her angry she might accuse him of something that hadn't happened. When Joseph reached for his schedule, she pulled it back with a playful smile. "You didn't answer my question."

"No," he said.

She batted her eyes at him. She was wearing so much makeup it looked like she was trying to shake off a few layers. "You don't even want to think about it?"

Other guy leaned across the desk to snatch the paper from her hand. He gave it to Joseph and held out his hand again. "Now mine," he said.

Joseph scurried to the door while he checked his final dates. He waited for the other guy before he stepped back into the hallway.

"Man, if Mr. D. wasn't such a troglodyte, we wouldn't have to go in there at all," other guy said. "Good luck with whatever you're doing next."

"Thanks. Good luck to you, too."

He understood what Joseph meant because he held up a hand with a wedding ring and said, "I have kryptonite," before he walked away.

Joseph kind of wanted to skip as he walked to his car. After the next few days, he'd be fully engaged in his dream job. The scary side of that would probably hit him as soon as he cashed his last paycheck. But for now, things were really looking wonderful.

4

"It's so awful, Mom."

"You can always come back and work for us," Emily's mom said through the phone.

"Are you suggesting you'd fire the person who replaced me?"

"Oh, no. But your father says she's not nearly as efficient as you were," she said. "You could help her out while we found some other things to fill your time."

Emily's parents would simply invent a job for her? If that wasn't the definition of spoiled, it was close. "No, thanks, Mom. I'm tough," Emily said. "Or at least I'm trying to be tough. I'm going to stick it out until I can figure out something better on my own."

"I saw the sweetest little girl today. Two years old. Told me all about how she was going to help with the new baby on the way."

"Aw." Emily did miss the little ones, even though she hadn't interacted with them much. But she knew her mom knew that and mentioned it at least partly to tempt her back.

"I can't wait to see babies who are related to me," her mom said. "Have you met anyone in Andauk?"

"Nice segue, Mom," Emily said sarcastically.

"And that was a nice dodge. *Have* you met anyone?"

Emily smiled because she immediately thought of Joseph Ziebert. She'd definitely met him. And she'd definitely ruined any chance she might have had so there was no point in telling her mom. "I'll let you know if I ever have a date."

"Hmm. Terrible job. No guys. Problems at your apartment. Your father wants to know what it would take for you to reconsider this move."

"I haven't hit it yet," Emily said. "The church is nice. I'm going to a festival tomorrow, and I'm even donating a cake."

"You're baking a cake?"

"It's in the oven as we speak." Emily made it sound much simpler than it actually was. She'd been about to mix up the cake when it occurred to her that she didn't yet own any cake pans. She wasn't in her mom's kitchen anymore. She made a second trip to the grocery store only to find it didn't carry pans. She drove to the next slightly larger town and found a pair of round cake pans. Then she returned home and got the cake in the oven. She decided to call her mom while it was baking.

"Are you planning to eat some of it?" her mom asked.

Emily scoffed. "Mom, how would it look if I donated a cake with a big bite out of it?"

"That's not what I meant." Emily could hear the frown in her mother's voice, as though it should have been obvious that she hadn't meant what she said. "Are you going to eat some of the treats available at the festival?"

"Maybe. I'm not sure you, either as my mom or as a nurse, should be encouraging me to eat garbage."

"Not garbage. A treat. You shouldn't deprive yourself of anything tasty on a quest for a perfect body that, by the way, doesn't exist."

Emily sighed. She'd heard this speech, or one like it, so many times. "I do treat myself occasionally, Mom. But you know for a while there I was living on fast food and candy. I thought I should start trying to eat more… more like a grownup."

The timer on Emily's phone started beeping loudly in her ear. She jerked it away to shut it off.

"Is that your cake?" her mom asked.

"Yeah." Emily held the phone to her ear with one hand and opened the oven door with the other. Something was wrong. She flipped on the oven light, and it stayed dark inside. "Uh, I gotta go so I can work on this."

"All right. Talk to you later, honey."

Emily tossed the phone onto a towel on her counter to concentrate on the oven. It didn't feel hot enough, and the cake was still liquidy in the middle. She flipped the light switch a few times. She turned the knob to off then back to cake cooking temperature. Nothing was happening. Had her oven just died in the middle of making a cake? In the middle of doing a favor for the guy who thought she was a moron? No. No. No. This was impossible.

Then Emily noticed that the clock on her microwave was also dark. Had the power gone out? Was that better? She still couldn't bake a cake. She rushed to the bedroom and turned on a light. It worked. Maybe it was just a fuse.

The landlord had shown her the fuse box one of the times he was there. He'd even said it had some issues. Maybe she could fix this. Though she'd never in her life opened a fuse box let alone touched anything inside one. She went to the hallway and tugged on its cover before she figured out that she needed to lift up the latch to open it. The inside was scary. Lots of knobs she knew nothing about except that they were somehow connected to electricity. The landlord had made it sound easy.

Her eyes began to read the labels down the side. AC, bathroom, kitchen 1, kitchen 2… She read all the labels before she backed up and zeroed in on the two for the kitchen. One of them was red. She put her finger on the switch and bit her lip as she moved it to the side. She didn't get electrocuted so that was a minor victory. She bit down even harder as she slid it back where it started. The only difference was that it was no longer red. Was that it?

She closed the fuse box and returned to the kitchen. The microwave was flashing at her. The oven light was on and the bottom was glowing with a promise of heat. Yes! Emily spun in a circle and did a quick jig. Her celebration halted as she began to worry about the cake again. How long did she need to bake a half-baked cake? Would it still taste okay? Would it be flat? Would anyone know which cake was the one she made?

Joseph would know. She was going to hand it to him, and he would know that she made it. He would know who won her cake. And if that person ever said to him, "I can't believe my luck. I got the worst cake at the festival," Joseph would know that Emily had made that terrible cake.

She didn't set a timer since she didn't know how much time to put on it. She checked the cake every minute or two as it cooked. By the time the center firmed up, she was convinced the whole thing was awful. Surely she'd seen other cakes puff up more. And if the texture didn't dampen the flavor, sitting in a lukewarm oven must have. As soon as it was cool enough, she dumped one of the pans onto a plate. It smelled good, but that had to be misleading. Emily broke a piece off the side to verify exactly how much the cake had been damaged by the break in baking.

She popped a bite into her mouth. Then she threw her head back and screamed at the ceiling. "Argh!" She glared at the cake. "You taste delicious. And I've ruined you anyway by taking a chunk out of the side."

She briefly considered whether or not she could cover that chunk with frosting. It couldn't be done. Not by her. She tossed the rest of the cake into the trash because she didn't need the temptation. She washed both the pans and set them out to dry while she ran to the store for another cake mix.

The second cake baked smoothly. Emily pulled a chair in front of the oven and watched it out of the corner of her eye while she read. She'd ordered a book about saints in the hope that she'd be able to contribute more on Fridays. Of course the book had arrived on a Saturday, but she was reading it now for the next week.

The cakes separated from the pans perfectly and the aroma of chocolate got even stronger in her apartment. Jessica had said the previous night that she was bringing a white cake. Gabriel, with Ruth's help, was going to make something called true gingerbread because he thought it would taste best with oat flour. Emily hadn't known what he was talking about except that he seemed to be saying he was a much better cook than she was. That was fine though. She didn't think she could go wrong with simple chocolate even if it came from a mix. Joseph had missed the meeting so she hadn't been able to hear his opinion on the subject. She hoped he liked chocolate.

The frosting was vanilla. Emily would have preferred more chocolate on the chocolate. But she was not going to eat this cake, and she wanted a nice presentation. Since she had no idea how to decorate a cake, she planned to cover it with sprinkles. The little balls of color would show up better against the white frosting.

She spread a coat of frosting on the bottom layer. When she added the top layer, it landed a bit crooked. Fortunately, she was able to slide it into place. Nothing was hanging over the edge. She scooped out a large dollop of frosting and began to spread it over the top. A potential problem began to appear. Not only did the sprinkles show up better in the white frosting but the dark cake crumbs did, too. The more Emily tried to spread frosting over those crumbs, the more crumbs she stirred up. She scooped out more frosting and now there were crumbs in the can. She kept trying to cover up the dark specks and kept creating more dark specks until she got so frustrated, she stabbed the knife right into the center of the cake.

She jumped back with her hands over her face. "What have I done to you?" she asked the cake.

It sat there with a knife sticking out of it like a murder victim.

Emily winced. Was there any way to salvage it now? She pulled the knife out slowly. It was completely coated with crumbling chocolate cake. She put that knife in the sink and got out a clean one. Very gingerly, she tried to spread frosting around the hole she'd made. There were so many crumbs. Maybe she could pretend she'd done that on purpose? Would anyone believe it was cookies and cream frosting? No. It looked terrible. It looked like a kindergartner had frosted the cake. Actually, a kindergartner probably could have done a better job.

Emily clapped her hands together to address someone other than the cake. "God... is there a message here? Are you trying to tell me I shouldn't have volunteered to do something to impress a guy? Because that wasn't the *only* reason. It's still a good cause, right?"

Shaking her head in dismay, Emily dumped the cake into the trash on top of the first cake she'd ruined. She cleaned up, then went to the store for the third time that day.

It appeared that Saturday afternoon was a popular time to visit the grocery store. Emily dodged the first customer before she even got through the doors. It was a woman pushing a shopping cart with three kids hanging on to the sides of it. There was a stab of jealousy that might not have been as sharp if Emily had been having a less miserable day. She wanted kids though. She wanted kids and all the miserable days that might come with them.

Emily went down the wrong aisle first and got trapped between two indecisive shoppers who didn't seem to have any idea their carts were blocking her in. Then she went and stood at the cake mixes for a moment. She asked herself which one she should ruin this time before she grabbed a third copy of the same. She picked up a can of chocolate frosting to go with it. So what if the sprinkles didn't look as pretty. Chocolate was delicious. Someone at that cake walk would appreciate that taste was the most important element of dessert.

The can slipped from her fingers and rolled across the floor. There was a tiny bit of comfort in knowing that she didn't only drop stuff in front of cute guys. She picked it up and carried an item in each hand to the end of the aisle where she nearly collided with a woman staring at her phone as she walked. She didn't even look up as Emily went around her.

There were two checkout lines. Naturally, Emily stepped into the shorter one. She fully expected it to be the slower line and was not disappointed. Depending on how she looked at it.

The cashier's voice carried back to her as she seemed to have a comment for every item she scanned. "The bananas are so green today, aren't they?"

"I wish they still made this cereal in the vanilla flavor. Did you ever try that?"

"Oh. This is my favorite peanut butter."

"How many sweet potatoes are in here?"

That seemed to be the first thing she said that got a response from the customer, a one-word response. She kept smiling and chatting as the groceries were bagged and paid for.

The next customer, an older man with thin hair, planted a heavy basket onto the conveyor belt.

"Look at all this cat food!" the cashier exclaimed. "How many do you have?"

His answer was too quiet for Emily to hear because she wasn't *trying* to hear.

The woman at the register spoke as though she was giving a presentation. It would have been hard not to hear. "No, how many cats?" she said. She continued after a pause, where she may or may not have gotten a response. "I had a cat for fourteen years. She died two months ago, and I still have to remind myself not to buy food for her." She was reading all the labels as she scanned the cans. "Some of these almost sound tempting," she said. "Salmon dreams? Sounds like a restaurant dish."

Emily was in the middle of a silent plea to God to let the chatter stop and the line move when she looked at the cashier, really looked at her. She had a wide clip on top of her head that appeared to be holding back the darker hair while the grays popped out. She was probably sixty or approaching it. The crow's feet around her eyes were pronounced. It was her smile that caught Emily's attention. It was strained. Was this woman having a miserable day, too? Or was she taking it all personally? Did she feel that no one wanted to stand around chitchatting in the checkout line because they didn't want to talk to her?

The man with all the cat food finished and the last customer before Emily stepped up. He looked to be in his thirties and had two kids with him, both girls. They were standing with their backs to the register discussing which candy bars they would buy if they were allowed to buy candy.

"You're smart to buy the meat when it's marked down," the cashier said. "This will be good for three or four days even if you don't freeze it."

The man nodded.

She continued scanning groceries. "Lots of cereal. Which of these is your favorite?" She raised her voice unnecessarily to direct her question to the girls. They still paid no attention. Their dad just shrugged.

"I like this unscented laundry soap, too. It's, uh…" She put it in the bagging area without finishing the thought because the man had turned around to check on his daughters. Then she raised her eyebrows as she shook a box of elbow pasta. "Macaroni and cheese?"

The man showed sudden, though still mild, interest. "Yes. My wife and I have been experimenting with different recipes. We can't seem to find one we all really like."

Her face lit up. "I'll give you my mother's recipe." She set the box down to rummage through a drawer under the register. She pulled out a roll of register tape, ripped off a few inches, then grabbed a pen. She completely stopped the checkout process to write out the recipe.

The man stared at the ceiling in an extended eye roll. Emily heard groaning and weight shifting behind her. But she found herself smiling. This wrong place, wrong time kindness was still kindness. Maybe the people behind her had somewhere to be, but Emily realized she wasn't in a hurry to get home and fail at making a cake again. She hoped this man and his family ended up enjoying the recipe. Then he might be more grateful than he sounded when he muttered a thank you.

Finally, it was Emily's turn and she was close enough to read the nametag. "Good afternoon, Maria," she said with a nod at the tag.

Maria smiled as she picked up the first item to scan. "Good afternoon to another chocolate cake fan." She froze as her eyes darted back and forth between Emily and the mix in her hand. "Is it my imagination or were you in here buying chocolate cake earlier today?"

"Guilty," Emily said. "I ruined the last one."

"Now how did you manage to ruin cake?"

"Half the top layer turned into crumbs when I tried to frost it. It wasn't pretty."

Maria let out a friendly laugh. "That's not ruined. A cake doesn't have to look good to taste good."

"I'd agree if it was for me, but…"

"Oh!" Maria nodded her understanding. "Did you let it cool first?"

"Yeah."

"All the way? You'll get more crumbs if the cake's even a little warm."

Emily had to admit she'd been a little impatient. "Maybe not," she said. "Thanks for the advice."

"You're welcome." She totaled the purchase and Emily thanked her again as she left.

When she returned to her apartment, Emily found that her oven was still on. How had she forgotten that? She was never going to prove to anyone that she could take care of herself if she burned her place down. She took a few deep breaths to relax and appreciate that no harm had been done this time. She concentrated on getting the recipe right, even getting down to eye level with the measuring cup. This cake was going to be good enough to eat no matter what. She checked it frequently as it cooked. Both layers rounded nicely, and they came out of the pans without sticking.

Time to let them cool thoroughly. Part of her thought she could just stand there and inhale the delightful aroma until they were ready to frost. Her stomach made a loud gurgling noise to protest that idea. It'd been doing that for a while. Between the multiple trips to the store and all the cake Emily had been messing up, it was 4:30 in the afternoon and she hadn't eaten since breakfast. It would be an excellent time to treat herself. Fortunately, as good as it smelled, she had no appetite for cake.

5

Emily had been wanting to try the burger place on Main Street since she moved to town. She'd heard it was good. Now that she was about to eat lunch and dinner at the same time, it wouldn't matter that one of those burgers likely had enough calories for two meals.

Main Street was pretty crowded on a Saturday. She had to park three blocks away from Burger Brothers. Despite the cold, she was fine with the extra steps. More exercise fit into her life improvement plan somewhere. She just hadn't figured out what kind of exercise she liked yet. She'd tried her dad's stationary bike for a while before she moved out. It was so boring. How could anyone ride a bike for thirty minutes thinking about nothing but going nowhere?

A building she walked past had paper covering the inside of the windows and no sign. Curious, she put her face up to the window and tried to see through a crack between two pieces of paper. It was dark inside, and she couldn't make out more than a lot of empty space.

"Hey! No peeking."

Emily jumped backwards at the deep voice.

"Sorry. Didn't mean to scare you." It was Joseph. Where had he come from?

"You didn't." A lie and they both knew it. Also, not what she meant to say. "I mean, I know you didn't mean to."

"Still sorry," he said.

She could sense an apologetic gesture with his hands even though they were inside the pockets of a nice black overcoat. He wore faded jeans and work boots underneath and the dark shadow of having skipped a day of shaving. The mixed appearance wasn't nearly as diverting as the general masculine appeal. "I, uh… Where'd you come from?" she asked.

A hand came out of his pocket to point to a narrow walkway between the buildings. "I parked in back."

"Oh." And just like that, Emily was out of things to say.

"You're not thinking about breaking into my building, are you?"

He was clearly teasing, and it made her laugh. "This is your building?"

"Yep."

"What's it gonna be?"

He smiled mysteriously. "A surprise."

The smile made her really warm. And stupid. She just smiled back without saying anything.

"I was just helping my mom bake a few cakes for the festival tomorrow," he said. "You were going to make one, right?"

She didn't want to talk about that disaster. "You were helping your mom? That was nice."

"It was real nice of me to help her with something I asked her to do," he said. Then followed the sarcastic comment with a yawn.

She was boring him. She could laugh at herself, turn the disaster into an entertaining story. "Well, I messed up the cake you asked me to make. Or my oven did, and I left it on."

Joseph wrinkled his forehead in confusion.

She didn't blame him. She had been there, and she still didn't understand what she'd just said.

"You burned it?" he asked.

She shook her head. "The oven went out because of a fuse so it didn't cook until I reset it and then it took so long and the interruption… I figured it must be damaged, like freezer burn only not, but I tasted it and it was fine. Except that I'd tasted it."

"What?" He still didn't understand. And he yawned again. And she could see that he was trying to cover a smile and a yawn. Now he was bored and laughing at her.

Emily fought her racing pulse to speak slower and more clearly. "A fuse broke and turned off my oven, apparently right after I put the cake in. I didn't notice until the timer went off. I got it hot again but was afraid the break had affected the taste so I cut off a little piece. Then even though it tasted good, I couldn't use it because I'd cut a chunk out of it."

"You could have covered that with frosting."

"No." She'd told enough of the story that she figured she might as well keep going. "Because I found out with the second cake that I have no skills at frosting either."

"What happened to the second cake?" He tipped his head forward and might have appeared genuinely interested if he hadn't yawned again.

"I stabbed it."

She got a good laugh with that pronouncement. But then he said, "What really happened?"

She had to look away from his amusement. "That's what really happened," she said. "I was getting crumbs mixed in the frosting all over the place and I got frustrated and I stabbed it."

"Okay." He stepped backwards. "Remind me not to make you angry."

"I only stab cakes," she said. "I promise."

He was yawning again. Even when she was coherent, she was boring him senseless.

"So, uh…" Joseph looked her up and down as though he was suddenly nervous. "Do you… do you have a cake for the festival or should I go back to my mom's house?"

"Oh, I have a cake," she answered quickly. "Or I will."

"You will?" He sounded doubtful.

Emily almost wanted to ask which of her confessions caused the most doubt. It was probably better that she didn't know. "I will," she repeated. "It's cooling right now. I just need to frost it when I get home. I will be more careful this time."

He nodded but didn't look convinced.

"I'll bring it tomorrow and then you'll see that… that it's edible." Best not to make any bold promises.

"I'm looking forward to that," he said with a smile. He also yawned again.

She really needed to let him go. She gestured down the street. "Well, I'm on my way to dinner."

"And I'm on my way to bed." He pointed at the paper-covered door. "Sorry about all the yawning. Didn't sleep well, and I've been up since two."

"Oh. Good night."

"See you tomorrow, Emily." He turned away as he took a set of keys from his pocket.

Emily had a new bounce in her step as she walked towards the striped awning of Burger Brothers, encouraged by that last bit of information. Joseph had been yawning because he was tired. Maybe. Her internal smile dimmed. She might still have been boring him. People could be tired and bored at the same time.

Thoughts of Joseph and things she wanted to kick herself for saying to him disappeared as she reached the restaurant door. There was a bright red help wanted sign taped to it. "Are you a sign from God?" she asked it.

Flipping burgers sounded like a step backward in her career evolution. But she made barely more than minimum wage at her current job. She'd willingly take a pay cut for a more pleasant atmosphere. She smiled at the sign. "I know what you're thinking. Don't get ahead of myself."

She grabbed the door handle to let herself in. First, she would have a meal there, see if she could get a feel for the place. Then, if it seemed comfortable, she'd ask about the job. Only if she liked the answers would she think about taking it. One step at a time.

Her first step halted on the threshold while her senses adjusted. It was louder than she expected, darker than she expected, and almost empty. Two rows of booths ran up and down the large space. There was a high counter along one wall where the only customer sat with a laptop. A long table crowded with chairs was on the other side. The music blaring through the speakers was upbeat bluegrass. It made Emily want to dance, except that dancing in a strange restaurant might be considered a mark against a future employee. She let the door close behind her and tried to figure out if there was a place to order or if she was supposed to wait for someone to show her to a seat.

A blur of color whipped up to her side and stopped just before crashing into her. "Welcome to Burger Brothers." The woman talking to her looked to be close to Emily's mom's age. She was round in the middle, curly on top, and her color and speed could be attributed to a flowery dress and bright green roller skates.

"Hi," Emily said.

"Go right up to the window to order, honey." The woman pointed to a register at the other end of the restaurant. "Chip will help you. He's my husband so I love him anyway." With that confusing statement, she pushed off and zipped towards some double doors. She yelled, "Dinner!" on her way.

Emily walked slowly towards the order window. It was about a three-foot square cut into the wall of wood paneling. The word order was printed on a sign above it. Another opening closer to the double doors was labeled pick up. Emily didn't see anyone through either. Her feet took smaller steps as she approached someone who was apparently loved anyway. That sounded ominous.

The music suddenly got quieter and little squares of moving lights appeared all around. Emily looked up to see that a spotlight was now shining on a disco ball. Interesting. When she turned back, there was a heavily moustached man with dark hair and eyebrows. His green shirt and white apron made her imagine asking him to rescue the princess. Then she imagined him not finding that the slightest bit amusing and banished the thought. He was frowning as though there wasn't much that he would find amusing.

"Hello," Emily said. She tried to offer a friendly smile.

He grunted and said, "You're a noob."

"Yeah. I've been wanting to try this place for a while."

"A while?" He raised an eyebrow as though she could have no excuse good enough for putting her visit off as long as a while.

Emily pinched her lips together to keep from smiling. Was she that nervous? Why was his surly attitude making her want to laugh?

"You're not going to make me explain to you what a burger is, are you?"

Oh, no. That was funnier. Emily tried to swallow her laugh and choked on it. She held her arm over her mouth as she started coughing, trying to keep her smile covered as well as the cough. "Excuse me," she said as she got control of herself.

Chip's moustache twitched. His eyes looked up and then back at her.

She followed his gaze. Now that she was close she could see that there was a menu above him. "Okay," she said. "Let me see."

She could see him slowly shaking his head at her out of the corner of her eye, and it was distracting. Coupled with the fact that she was still trying not to laugh made it really hard to concentrate on the menu.

A strong whiff of body odor made her realize that someone had gotten in line behind her. She fought the urge to wrinkle her nose as she nodded a greeting to the new arrival. He was a much older man with scraggly hair and weathered skin. Instead of a jacket, he appeared to be wearing every piece of clothing that he owned. Multiple collars and sleeves stuck out haphazardly with some hems more frayed than others.

Despite the many layers, Emily could still tell that he was very thin and somewhat frail-looking. The smell made her want to back away, but it was mixed with an honest desire to be polite as she said, "I don't know what I want yet so you can go first."

The man smiled and put a hand on his heart before he bent into a deep bow.

Chip remained stony-faced as he greeted the man. "How's it going, Jojo?"

The older man, Jojo, suddenly threw both arms out to the sides and waved them up and down.

"Hungry today, huh?"

Jojo nodded vigorously.

"Well?" Chip pointed at the menu.

Jojo put his hands together, but Emily couldn't tell what sort of gesture he was making.

"You gotta speak up," Chip said.

All humor at the man's demeanor disappeared. Emily couldn't believe he would say something so rude to a man who clearly could not speak.

Jojo just pointed at the sign again. This time he used two fingers.

"Oh. Double cheeseburger?"

The older man nodded and brushed one hand over the other as though trying to rub something off.

"What do you want me to leave off it?"

Jojo drew a circle in the air with his finger.

"I don't know what that means," Chip said, "and my burgers are perfect the way they are."

Jojo repeated the same circular motion.

Chip sighed. "All right. I'll list the ingredients. Stop me when I get to what you don't what. Mustard. Ketchup. Pickles. Onions."

The hand that Jojo raised appeared to be waving goodbye to the onions.

"Onions? Really?" Chip asked. "You know you can't smell any worse."

Emily felt her mouth drop open at that comment. Who did this Chip guy think he was?

"Be ready in a minute." Chip tipped his head to the side as he spoke to indicate that Jojo should move over for her to place an order.

Emily stepped up to give the man a piece of her mind. She hesitated though because she didn't know if doing so in front of Jojo might embarrass him. He didn't seem bothered by the treatment. He just smiled at both of them.

Then something occurred to Emily. Jojo hadn't paid for his food. More importantly, he didn't seem to have been expecting to pay for his food. The two men must have some sort of established relationship, one that allowed a little leeway on manners. If it also included giving a free meal to a man who looked like he could use one, maybe she shouldn't be so quick to criticize it.

"Have you made up your mind?" Chip asked.

"Not yet."

He turned his head towards the menu then back at her with a look that suggested it should not be that difficult to choose.

All of a sudden, his expression caused her to fight another smile. She must be in an odd mood to have Mr. Grouch be so entertaining. "Can you tell me what's on your standard cheeseburger?" she asked.

He listed the ingredients as though he was bored.

She pressed her lips tighter as she nodded. "Okay. I'll have that."

"Do you want it well done or well done?"

That's when she lost it, just completely cracked up for a few seconds. She drew in a calming breath and rubbed her hand over her face. "Well done," she said. "And maybe some water."

There was more twitching of the moustache. "*Maybe* you want water?"

"Yes, I'll have water. Cheeseburger and water. That's all."

He told her the price, which she handed over. Then he pointed behind her. "Go sit somewhere."

A family with young children came in as she settled herself in a booth. The woman on roller skates zipped from the kitchen to greet them. They addressed her as Paula. Paula did a short moonwalk-like backwards skate before she turned around and disappeared through the double doors again. Several more customers had gotten in line by the time the family finished ordering.

"Here you go, Jojo." The woman named Paula handed something wrapped in white paper through the pickup window.

Jojo made a surprisingly graceful bow as he took it. Then he made a beeline for the exit.

Paula came out with Emily's order a minute later. "This look right?" she asked.

It looked like a cheeseburger so Emily nodded. She ate it

slowly, partly because it tasted fabulous and she wanted to savor it. She also took her time to study her surroundings. Paula always had a friendly smile even if some of her skate tricks were sad. The place stayed busy. A couple of times, she heard other voices coming from the kitchen. They were shouting to be heard but not yelling at each other. She noticed there were even a couple of customers for whom Chip dropped the grouchy act, which assured her that it was an act. He told people they were making terrible decisions with their special orders, but he still gave them exactly what they wanted.

After an hour or so, Emily decided that she had seen enough. She waited for a break in the line of customers and then returned to the order window. Chip stared at her expectantly.

"Hi," she said. "I noticed you have a help wanted sign in the front window."

He turned around without saying a word and grabbed a sheet of paper from somewhere behind him. He slapped it on the counter and said, "Fill that out. Then come talk to me."

It was an application. She picked it up and said, "Thank you."

Chip gave her a random and unexpected salute.

She went back to her seat and dug through her bag for a pen. The form wasn't difficult to complete. She still expected to be sitting with it for some time because a mob of people had just walked in the door. Emily began to wonder if perhaps Chip hadn't meant come talk to him *tonight*. It didn't look as though he would be available in the near future. She was also taking up valuable real estate as customers were looking for places to sit.

But despite Emily's intention to wait for details, she'd already convinced herself that she wanted this job. If the boss wanted to talk to her tonight and she left, that would be a strike against her. She decided to get in the order line again. When she got to the front, she'd hand him the application and ask what time she could talk to him the next day. She hadn't been in the line long when Chip made eye contact with her. He pointed at her, then pointed at the doors to the kitchen. Was she supposed to go back there?

She walked slowly in that direction. As she did so, she saw a younger man with a beard take Chip's place at the register. Chip popped out the doors just before she reached them and motioned impatiently for her to follow. He led her through those double doors. Paula gave her a thumbs up as she rolled past to exit through the same doors.

They entered a small office at the very back. It had a desk and several chairs, but Chip didn't take a seat or offer one to Emily. He simply held out his hand for the paperwork.

She stood silently as he skimmed the information. Something on the page made him smirk for a second. "Chuck hurt his back, that's my brother, and has been working less. Now he thinks he wants to retire altogether." Chip looked up from the paper. "He's a lot older than me, by the way."

Emily nodded. That seemed to be an important point.

"I need someone who is flexible. You need to be willing to man the grill or chop lettuce or take orders or basically do whatever I tell you. But you will not do anything before you've been properly instructed." He said this last bit as though it was a warning.

Emily was grateful to know she wouldn't be expected to figure anything out on her own. "Yes," she said. "I can be flexible and obedient."

He frowned at that and squinted his brushy eyebrows together.

"Is that the wrong answer?" she asked.

He frowned deeper. "It probably won't be more than thirty hours a week to start, but it might be more later if you prove yourself useful."

Emily frowned a little herself. But then she found out that the hourly wage was better than her current one. Even with fewer hours, it would be a small cut. And she was optimistic that these hours would be more pleasant. "Okay," she said.

"Okay?" Chip let his eyes bore into hers. "I say jump, you say?"

"How high?"

He pointed at the door behind her. The interview was apparently over.

6

Joseph recognized the back of her head when she turned to the side for a moment. Her hair was in a pair of very neat and complicated-looking braids down the back of her head. It was quite a contrast to the previous day when half of it was falling out of a ponytail with a bit of something white in it that, after hearing about her day, he guessed was frosting.

Both days, she was beautiful. He'd been drawn to Emily since the first time they met, when she'd arrived for a meeting as it was ending. There was something special about her. The clumsy streak and the perpetually confused expression were as appealing as her nice shape. She looked like a woman Joseph could take care of, a woman he could possibly spend the rest of his life taking care of. If she let him.

This was not to suggest he in any way thought she was helpless. He was certain she could get along just fine without him. But maybe there was room for him to make her life more than fine. He'd like to try.

It was an impulse he was going to need to keep in check because he didn't want to just ask her to dinner. He wanted to ask if they could go somewhere to talk for hours so he could start learning everything there was to know about her. A lengthy interview was probably not her idea of Prince Charming. There was a voice in the back of his head whispering that Emily could be the woman he'd been waiting for and that it was time to stop waiting. Those were dangerous thoughts to have about someone he didn't know. That was why he was in a hurry to begin to know her.

If he hadn't been wedged between his dad and his brother when he spotted her, he might have jumped up to move forward in the church to sit next to her. Perhaps it was a good thing that he was stuck with family. Except that she was sitting all by herself. She might appreciate the company. From the man who was practically a stranger? You could sit by strangers in a church though. In fact, it was encouraged and welcoming. But it wasn't as though he could talk to her during the Mass. He'd only be distracted by the physical appeal and frustrated by questions he couldn't ask. It was good that he had to stay where he was. But it was still frustrating.

Joseph was relieved when the congregation stood for the opening hymn. It obstructed his view of the woman who was messing with his head something awful. He wished he had some idea whether or not that was a good sign. He tried to catch her eye as he passed after communion. Her pretty eyes were closed in prayer. One more thing that made her seem like a good match, as if he needed the ammunition.

He lost sight of Emily when it was time to leave. He'd been doing too well pretending not to look at her and missed which direction she headed.

Isaac noticed the search. "Are you looking for someone?" he asked.

"Emily," Joseph said.

"Ah." Isaac didn't help look for her. He only nodded as though a lot of questions had been answered by the one word.

Joseph gave up fairly quickly. He was going to see her at the festival soon anyway. And they'd be able to talk more if his family wasn't hovering. He followed his parents to their house for a quick lunch. The meal itself wasn't rushed at all, but they normally spent the afternoon socializing and wouldn't have time that Sunday. Several of them had been drafted for various festival events. Ella excused herself through Ruth since there would be no time for games or talking. Adam wasn't there, but no one expected him to be there. He did at least text their dad that he wouldn't make it. No excuse given.

Joseph was the first to leave. It took a few trips to get all the cakes to his car. He planned to drive very carefully. Ruth followed him out the back door as he left with the one his mom had covered in coconut. She hadn't put on a coat and was bouncing up and down in the cold. "Wait," she said. "Before you go, can we have an awkward conversation?"

"Sure," he said. "I was just thinking about how much I wanted to have an awkward conversation with my sister."

She chuckled at the sarcasm. "I'll get to the point. Are you interested in Ella?"

"No."

"She's really nice, you know."

"I didn't say I had anything against her, and you said we should get to the point."

Ruth rubbed her hands together as she shivered. "Well, that's good actually. She was afraid you might be feeling pressure to…uh…" She read something on his face. It was either relief that it sounded as though Ella wasn't interested in him either or impatience to deliver the cake he was holding. "So anyway, you're fine with her joining us on Sunday but have no intention of asking her out?"

"Yep."

"Okay." She turned around and hurried into the house.

Though it felt a bit childish to communicate through his sister, that conversation had probably been less awkward and shorter than talking directly to Ella. He quickly forgot about it to focus on the festival. Joseph spotted a few flurries in the air on the short drive. He wasn't surprised to find everything set up indoors. Kiddie games that were in the parking lot when the weather was less nippy lined the school hallway.

Fortunately, the gym was near the entrance. He didn't have to repeatedly navigate the crowds while carrying fragile desserts. He put the cakes he brought with the others and made a mental note of which one he would want. The cake walk seemed ready to go.

Joseph wondered if Mrs. Donnelly had asked him to come early just to be sure he wasn't late. She might also have been covering her bases in case other setup took longer than expected. Joseph wouldn't mind being early at all if Emily would arrive. He could spend the time he wasn't setting up trying to talk to her.

First he saw Mr. and Mrs. McGrady walking up, each with a fancy cake in hand. They were a very cute old couple who always seemed to be together. About the only thing Joseph knew about them was that they were cute. Though now he knew that at least one of them was good with frosting. One cake had elaborate swirls of white frosting covered with a dusting of cocoa powder. The other had light green frosting barely visible through all the different colored flowers.

"Those look amazing," he said.

Mr. McGrady tipped his head towards his wife. "It's all her," he said.

She smiled proudly. "A cake really only needs to taste good, but I do love an excuse to make them pretty."

"What flavors are the cakes?" Joseph asked.

"Both white," she said.

He nodded and made sure they were displayed at the front of

the table to attract visitors. Then he waved to the old couple and looked around for Emily.

And there she was. The red bag she carried stood out in the sea of activity, but he would have seen her anyway. The bag had slipped to her elbow. There was a chocolate cake in her hands. She'd stopped just inside the doorway and her eyes searched the room looking generally lost. Then they found Joseph, and she smiled. She smiled right at him as though she'd never been gladder to see anyone.

He kind of wanted to leap over the table to help her carry that cake. He waited for her to approach. "Hi," he said. "That looks good."

"Third time's the charm."

"The cake is chocolate, too?"

"Yeah." She bit the side of her lip. "Is that okay?"

"Definitely. I just need to be able to tell anyone who asks. You can put it right over here." He gestured to a place he'd saved in anticipation.

"Joseph?" Another woman approached the table as Emily set her plate down.

"Yes?" he said. The new woman looked familiar, but it took him a moment to place her. "Oh, Natalie, right?"

She smiled at the recognition. "Do you have a minute?"

He glanced at Emily. "Yeah, what's up?" Natalie had been in his class in high school. They hadn't known each other well and hadn't spoken since. She probably just wanted to ask a quick question, and he could get right back to Emily.

"Mrs. Wellington told me about the new gym you plan to open," Natalie said, "and I want to run an idea by you."

"Okay." Joseph was all ears now.

"Did you know that I'm teaching the art classes at the high school now?"

"No, I hadn't heard that."

Natalie smiled proudly. "This is my third year."

"Congratulations," Joseph said. "It looks like something you enjoy."

"I do, but..." She had really long blond hair over her shoulders that she used both hands to gather and drop behind her as though getting it out of the way for the important thing she had to say. "My students keep asking me to find a way for them to display some of their work. I've asked some of the local businesses and some out-of-town places as well, and I'm running out of ideas. But then Mrs. Wellington was telling me that you plan to have a track for walking or jogging and that might be perfect."

She held her hands up, and her eyes grew wider. "Wouldn't it be great if you could vary the scenery for your guests without having to do anything? If you'd just let us have a little wall space, I could come in maybe once a month to hang new pictures. What do you think?"

Joseph didn't know what he thought. He was mentally chewing on the idea.

"You don't look like you hate the idea," Natalie said.

"I don't hate it." He could say that much. "One thought I have is that some of the art could be damaged – accidentally, I would hope – but like if a ball bounces against it or something. That might tear or smudge it."

"I hadn't thought of that," Natalie said, though she didn't appear less determined to convince him.

"And I'm not sure off the top of my head where we would put them. I planned to keep the walls mostly plain on purpose because... Have you ever been somewhere where there's a poster on the wall and you can't help but read it over and over because it happens to be in front of you, and it's super annoying? Even if it's not a bad poster, just reading it so much?"

She threw her head back to laugh before he'd finished explaining. "I know what you mean," she said. "There are things in the school hallway that I have read sooo many times. I promise to try to remember not to bring any art with words on it."

She was looking at him expectantly. Joseph had been working on and planning this venture for so long he wasn't ready to make any snap decisions, even if it did sound like a good idea. "Well, I don't open for almost two months anyway so give me a chance to think about it with the walls in question in front of me, then I'll let you know."

"Absolutely," she said. "Give me your phone so I can put my number in it. Make sure you call me at least a week before you open so I'll have time to get the first batch of pictures up." She gave him a fawning smile as she entered her number.

Joseph laughed at her eagerness as he took his phone back. It did feel great that most of the people he talked to were excited about the business idea. Even his mom, once she got over the irritation of not being told sooner, had been supportive and encouraging. He really hoped the good will would translate into income.

He put aside the reverie to focus on where he was. People had begun to gather to look at the cakes. Emily was not among them. His eyes widened the search to some nearby craft vendors and those on the other side of the gym. No sign of her. He thought for sure she'd stick around for a while after dropping off the cake. Of course even if she did, he was stuck where he was until he gave away a lot of cakes.

There was no one around to tell him he couldn't start selling tickets a few minutes early. He asked those in front of him to go ahead and form a line for the first round.

He still finished right around 3 o'clock. He was wondering what to do next when a pair of teenage boys showed up. They said

Mrs. Donnelly sent them to clear the area for some square dancing and that Joseph should take the cash bag to the school office. He happily left them to the cleanup.

There were four elderly women in the office sitting around a card table littered with envelopes, scribbled pieces of paper, calculators and stacks of money.

"Proceeds from the cake walk," he said, holding up the bag uncertainly.

"Right here, hon." The closest woman held out her hand to take it.

Another woman picked up a pen. "Ziebert, right?" she asked. "What's your first name again?"

None of them looked up again after she made a note of his name so he figured he was free to go. Relieved of his volunteer duty, he wandered the festival. He saw his dad and Gabriel's dad – the families had been friends a long time – getting ready to roast chickens. His mom was helping with a duck pond. Ruth and Ella were selling popcorn. He did not find Emily anywhere. Just when he was thinking he'd give up and go home, Mrs. Donnelly found him.

"How'd the cakes go?" she asked.

"Great. Gave away all of them and only a few rounds weren't full."

"Perfect." She pushed her glasses down her nose to see over them. "You're not doing anything right now, are you?"

"Uh, no," he admitted, which he knew meant he was about to be doing something.

"I'm in a bind," she said. "We've had a few volunteers not show up. I drafted a young woman to help out behind the fishing game, but she said she could only stay until three. It's nearly 3:30 now so I really need someone to relieve her. Can you help us both out?"

Mrs. Donnelly wasn't what he'd picture as a damsel in distress, but her request tugged at the same instinct. "Yeah, I guess," he said.

"Thank you." She pushed her glasses up and motioned with the same hand for him to follow her. They walked down a hall and stopped in front of a panel mobbed with kids where she began to give instructions. "We have two volunteers out front selling tickets and helping kids get their prizes off the hooks. We need you to go behind the screen to attach the prizes. We're trying to keep the odds about one in three or one in four, but mix it up however you like. Just attach a prize, then give a little tug. Or pause and tug for no prize. We'll wrap up at five or when you run out of things to give away. Any questions?"

"No," he said. "I think I got it."

"Thanks again. Go tell the other volunteer she can go home." With that, Mrs. Donnelly turned around and walked off like a woman on a mission. That was exactly what she was.

Joseph headed towards the screen ready to make someone's day. He hoped he'd be able to switch with her without interrupting the game. Then he stopped hoping that and wished he could interrupt the game permanently so he could talk to Emily instead of replacing her. "Hello," he said.

"Joseph!" Her smile nearly knocked him over with how happy she looked to see him. Of course, she would've looked just as happy to see anyone who was there to relieve her.

"So you're the nice young lady Mrs. Donnelly drafted?"

"Guilty. Or, uh…" She wrinkled her nose as though that wasn't what she meant to say. Then she shrugged and said, "It's me."

"I know you have to go," he said, "but do you have any advice or anything I need to know first?"

"I have to go?" she repeated. "Oh, right. Well, these are the prizes." She waved her hand at some boxes then tugged a hook hanging near her before she picked up something to attach to another one. The boxes contained mostly candy with a few rubber bracelets and other trinkets. "There's tape here for anything that doesn't hook easily."

"Okay." He wanted to think of questions he could ask, but she would not thank him for wasting her time.

Another hook dropped over the screen and landed on Emily's head. "I'd tell you to watch out for the hooks so they don't get caught in your hair," she said, "but I don't think you'll have the same trouble I have." She winced as she untangled the tiny piece of plastic from the loops of her braid.

"Yeah, I think I'll be okay there."

She stood and gestured to the chair. "I guess you should take over."

He sat and tugged on the closest hook. He tugged on another and fished around in a box of goodies for something that looked easy to hook.

"Based on the cheers," Emily said, "those light up things have been pretty popular."

Joseph nodded.

"And... um... the licorice hooks easier than you might expect." After a pause she added, "I mean, at first I was trying to balance it with the hook right in the middle but a couple of sloppy ones didn't fall off so..."

It didn't sound as though Emily was in any hurry to leave. Maybe she'd rescheduled something while she was waiting. Maybe she'd already missed it. Maybe Joseph was grasping at anything that might make her willing to stay and work with him. He looked up, ready to ask and ready to vacate the chair if she could stay.

"Well, bye," she said first and grabbed her bag and coat from the floor. She disappeared around the corner with any chance this volunteer activity would be enjoyable.

Joseph sighed and returned his eyes to the blank wall of cardboard. There were no hooks waiting. And then a little piece of hard plastic dropped on his head. Ow. He was going to have to watch out for them even if they wouldn't get tangled in his hair.

7

Of course there was a line for the bathroom. Emily didn't even really need a bathroom. She only needed to give herself an excuse to run away from Joseph. The man had a knack for throwing her off balance, and that was something she usually managed to do without help.

She was determined to have a conversation with him where she did not humiliate herself. That had been her plan for the day. She brought the cake to him with an intent to offer her assistance. Even if she only provided company, it would be a chance for the two of them to get to know each other better. She knew she hadn't done anything to spark any romantic interest, but Joseph looked at her as though she had. She needed to spend enough time with him to figure out if his eyes were so attractive they made her see things that weren't there or if he actually saw something in her.

But that other woman had shown up when Emily had barely had a chance to say hello. Some vicious instinct that she didn't know she had made Emily look the woman up and down to catalog flaws. She had a double chin and many pimples she was trying to cover with thick makeup. Her pants squeezed her middle like a string around a tube of frosting.

Emily turned her back on the table and the nasty jealous feeling. She walked a few steps, letting her eyes float across some Christmas-themed needlework for sale, letting go of those feelings she didn't like. It wasn't easy to get control of herself, but when she turned back a little later and saw the woman laughing while Joseph took her phone number, she wasn't angry. Emily felt only disappointment. It wasn't better even if it was healthier.

She left the gym then, thinking she'd just go home. A quick change of heart made her stay. Joseph Ziebert was a nice guy, and she was going to continue trying to be his friend. She needed friends. She was new in town and couldn't afford to burn any bridges, even if it didn't appear to be a bridge to happily ever after.

The gym had been right behind her, but Emily never made it back inside. A woman with the air of someone in charge had redirected her to the fishing game. Emily told the first plastic hook that landed on her head that the coerced volunteering was likely penance for the uncharitable thoughts she'd had towards a woman whose only crime was knowing Joseph's name.

Despite what had begun feeling like an exile behind the finishing pond, Emily had a little fun back there. She heard a few kids speculating on how the game worked and an older, more astute child loudly telling the pond what he hoped to receive.

Her mood was fairly cheery when Joseph suddenly appeared behind the screen with her. For one glorious second, she'd thought he had sought her out, that he'd been looking for her. Then he mentioned how she needed to go and realized he'd only been assigned to take her place. She already wished she'd handled the situation better. She should have told him she didn't need to leave, but then he probably would have left. And she didn't want him to think she'd lied to the woman who recruited her.

It was finally Emily's turn in the bathroom. She glanced up at the mirror while she washed her hands, then did a double take. Her formerly neat braids had several loose pieces of hair sticking up. Those fishing hooks had done more damage than she'd thought. Or maybe she had done the damage trying to remove them. Either way, her hair was a mess. She tried to use her fingers to push the sticking up parts under the flatter parts. It wasn't working. She pulled out both rubber bands and combed her fingers through her hair to remove the braids entirely.

Should she redo them? Aside from the other people waiting to use the sink, her hair looked fine down. Emily slipped the rubber bands onto her wrist and returned to the hall. She glanced around, trying to decide if she was done with this festival. The only thing she knew for sure was that her eyes were seeking out that fishing game in the corner far more than anything else. She was tempted to return to it.

She didn't know what kind of arm-twisting it had taken to get Joseph to do that job. Maybe he didn't have anything better to do. Maybe he'd stay and talk to her. Maybe they'd have fun together. Maybe she'd just embarrass herself again. Emily had done a few stupid things in her life. Would going back to chat with Joseph be one of them?

There was only one way to find out. Her legs were carrying her towards the answer before she could talk herself out of it. She knew it was a bad idea. She didn't have to prove it was a bad idea. Why was she trying to prove it was a bad idea? Why was the sky blue? That was an easier question, but Emily didn't have time to answer either before she was back behind the screen and face to face with Joseph.

"Did you forget something?" He looked around for what it could be.

"No, I thought... you might like some company." She dropped her stuff and took a seat on the floor before he could offer her the chair. She was afraid that if he stood up he would leave. He might leave anyway, but she thought she'd try to do whatever she could to discourage it.

"Would you rather have the chair?" he asked.

"No. Please stay where you are." *Please.*

There were no waiting fish hooks at the moment and the coaxing they heard through the cardboard wall sounded like a very small kid trying to get one over. Joseph got a piece of candy ready. The effort was going to be rewarded. Maybe Emily's was, too, because he hadn't gotten up to leave. He glanced over at her as he said, "What happened to your, um, thing?"

Well, that was a nice change. Emily marveled at someone else asking an incoherent question before she said, "My what?"

He smiled mostly with his eyes. She got the impression that he wasn't laughing at the hook that just barely made it over the top or the one that sailed over after it. "Your reason for needing to leave at three," he said.

She'd expected him to immediately ask why she didn't have to leave after all so it was probably her fault that she hadn't understood. "Oh, well, I didn't exactly say I needed to leave. She asked if I could cover it until three, and I told her it would be great if someone else took over then since I kind of wanted to be somewhere else."

"Where did you want to be?"

Of course that would be the next question. She plastered on a confident, casual smile. "That's what time the cake walk was supposed to end. I wanted to ask you how it went."

"Really?" he said. There was a hopeful twinge in his voice. Or at least Emily heard one. Was it really there or were her ears telling her what she wanted to hear? It was probably just the cozy space where they were keeping their voices low.

"I did spend a lot of yesterday thinking about and working on cakes," she said. "You can't blame me for being curious about how everything turned out."

"Your cake was…" Joseph was momentarily distracted as all three hooks descended at once. "Yours was chosen pretty early. Chocolate was a good call."

"Thanks," she said. "Some of the others looked kind of fancy."

"Yeah, some of the kids were into the heavily decorated ones, but the adults seemed more interested in taste."

"Did everything go smoothly?"

He raised his eyebrows. "There was one minor incident. I called a number that a kid was on and the kid next to him shoved him off the square to take it over."

"Oh, no. How did you handle that?"

"I didn't have time to think what I would have done before their mom intervened. Apparently, the boys were siblings. She jumped in and told them she was going to pick the cake and that they had to be real good the rest of the day to get any."

"Interesting," Emily said. "That's like a threat and a bribe."

Joseph smiled. "I suspect it worked. Nothing motivates a kid like the idea that your sibling might get something you don't."

"Unfortunately, that's not something I know much about."

"You don't have any siblings?"

Emily shook her head. "My mom had some… trouble after I was born. She wasn't able to have any more kids."

"I'm sorry."

"Honestly, I'd feel sorrier if she didn't use that as her justification for bugging me about grandkids."

"Hmm." Joseph looked thoughtful while he decided which hook was getting the next piece of candy. That decision wasn't difficult, but he was distracted by their conversation. "When you say bugging you about grandkids, you mean…"

"I mean she brings it up every chance she gets," Emily said. "It's like she sees a kid walking down the street and says, 'Oh, by the way, when are you going to have some of those?'"

Joseph enjoyed her impression and that made Emily feel good. She reached over and tugged a hook.

"How do you know I wasn't going to put candy on that one?"

"I did this for an hour before you got here," she said. "I'm the expert."

"Really?"

"And you're not doing candy next. You're going to give one of those stretchy bracelets."

He cocked his head to the side. "So you're an expert and a mind-reader?"

"No," she said. The teasing was going well so she got a bit bolder. "I didn't read your mind. I know you're going to give a bracelet next because I just told you to."

He let out a short laugh of surprise. Then he picked up a yellow bracelet in one hand and a piece of candy in the other. He moved them up and down as though weighing which one to use. He watched Emily's reaction as he secured the bracelet and signaled the hook to be taken away.

She tried to look as though it was so expected it didn't matter. The smile pulling on her lips was probably giving her away.

"When your mom is hinting about grandchildren," Joseph began, stressing the word hinting as an obvious understatement, "is she hinting for a whole passel of them or just grandchildren in general?"

Numbers had not been mentioned. "I think she'd be happy with any, but it does seem to be plural whenever she talks about it."

"What do you think of that?" he asked.

"I'm used to it." Emily smiled as she said it. "I know my parents mean well with all their suggestions for my life."

He nodded and shook his head at the same time. "I meant what do you think about providing those grandchildren?"

"Oh, do I..." She kind of shrugged. "I'm not there yet. I want kids, but I think it'd be dangerous for me to spend too much time thinking about it until I have other parts of my life figured out."

"Other parts?" he said thoughtfully. He rewarded a couple of kids while he considered what to say. "Is that something your mom tries to help... I assume she'd like you to get married first?"

"Yes to all of the above," Emily said.

Joseph eyed her strangely. He seemed to enjoy the answer even though he didn't understand it.

"Yes, my parents want me to get married. Yes, they make lots of suggestions on what to look for in a guy. Yes, they have even tried to set me up with one or two specific suggestions. Yes, they think it should happen soon. I have already been told that I'm not getting any younger."

He laughed. "You're twenty-six, right?"

"Yeah."

"Imagine if you were thirty."

Emily had imagined that. "It's a scary thought," she said.

"I know." His eyes suddenly held less humor. "I'm almost there."

"Sorry."

He shrugged and brought back the teasing tone. "What sort of qualities are you supposed to be looking for?"

"Oddly enough, they've never mentioned what he should look like."

"Hmm." Joseph gave a little tug on one of the lines while the subject tugged on Emily's nerves.

She would probably start blushing if she tried to describe her dream guy while looking at a candidate for the position.

"How will you know when you've found him if you don't know what he looks like?"

"That's a good question," she said.

"I suppose… that you'd have to spend a lot of time with him to find out about the less visible qualities."

Emily nodded. "I suppose so." She picked up a piece of candy for the next hook. She was close enough to flirting with a guy who'd just given his number to someone else that she wanted to boost the pretense of being there to help the church.

"And what are some of those qualities?"

"Well, my dad likes to tease me that he's going to be someone who likes classical music."

That got Joseph's attention. He stared at her as a hook landed on his head. He gave it a look of fake annoyance before he sent it back. "What does classical music have to do with it?"

"It's his way of reminding me to look for what's important. He says that a husband and wife can like different types of books and even root for rival sports teams. But if one has a strong faith that the other mocks, that won't work. If I fall for a guy who loves to go out and party and I'm a homebody, that'll be hard."

"Okay," he said. "But why classical music?"

"My dad likes it." She could picture him pretending to conduct the music blaring through the house stereo. "I'm always giving him a hard time about how awful it is – or I was when I lived there – and he would say someday I'll end up with a guy who likes it because he reminds me of my dad."

Joseph nodded.

They reached for the same hook at the same time. Almost the same time. Emily was a second slower and ended up with her hand over the back of his. His skin was rough and warm. She pulled her hand away with an uneasy feeling that it hadn't been fast enough. Had she run her fingers over his or was the fraction of a second enough to leave such a strong impression.

His eyes seemed to linger on her hand, which confirmed her suspicion that the touch had been longer than an instant. Then he cleared his throat and started on a new, though related, topic. "Your dad is a pediatrician, right?"

"Yeah."

"And he wanted you to be one?"

It seemed that Joseph had been paying attention to her embarrassingly lengthy speech. "Yes," Emily said.

"Did you consider a different field of medicine? Or becoming a nurse like your mom?"

"Not really," she said. "By the time I'd decided against pediatrician, I knew the things I didn't like would apply to all areas."

"What was it you didn't like about working… You said you were doing insurance paperwork?"

"That was a lot of it."

"Boring?" Joseph asked hesitantly.

Then Emily hesitated. "No," she said meekly. "Maybe I'm nerdy, but the paperwork didn't bore me. I kind of enjoyed matching up the codes and making sure all the details were straight."

"You're a detail person?" He looked as though he was trying not to laugh.

"Why is that funny?" she asked.

"I don't know." His face got more serious as he looked at her inquisitively. "Something about you doesn't say detail person to me. It's an intriguing contradiction."

Emily's hopes raised at being called intriguing, though that wasn't necessarily good. Her dad had come across a few intriguing medical conditions.

"What was it you didn't like then?" Joseph asked.

"I'm really not sure. I don't think it was the job itself so much as the fact that my parents handed it to me." Emily chose her words slowly. "I realized that I... wasn't happy. Mostly because I wasn't taking care of myself. I was eating junk food and gaining weight and sleeping too much."

"Sleeping too much?"

"Yeah. I... I think sometimes I was going to bed early just to end the day sooner."

His brown eyes shone with compassion. "Are you better?"

"I'm getting there," she said. And it felt like the truth. "Since I didn't really know why I wasn't happy, I thought I'd fix myself in reverse. Start eating better, get healthier, then see what else I wanted to change. My parents approved of the efforts and maybe this makes me sound like a rebellious adolescent, but their approval bothered me. I wanted to make sure I was making myself healthier for me. I needed them to not be looking over my shoulder to do that."

"Hence the drastic changes to your job and home," Joseph said.

"Drastic?" Emily raised an eyebrow. "That's what my dad said. He asked why I couldn't keep the job and just move out."

"And?" Joseph raised an eyebrow right back.

"I don't know." She was startled out of thinking of a better answer when an older woman popped her head around the corner.

"It's nearly five," the woman said. "How are we looking on prizes?"

"There's plenty left," Joseph told her. They'd consolidated everything to one small box, but it was nearly full.

"We don't have to use them all," she said. "The teachers can use what's left for classroom prize boxes, but let's increase the odds for the last few minutes."

"Aye, aye," Joseph said.

Emily smiled at his playful response, but she felt a sudden panic at the time being almost over. It had gone so quickly. And she'd talked about herself the whole time. He must think her incredibly self-centered. She began to twist her hands together nervously. He hadn't left, and she'd still done nothing positive with their time together.

"Emily?" he said. It sounded as though he was trying to get her attention.

She was two feet away. Did she look as distracted as she felt? "Yes?"

"Since we're almost done here, would you be willing to extend our time together. Like maybe over dinner?"

"Now?"

"I would have eaten already if I was home. Getting up early for work makes me want to eat early even on the days I don't drive."

"Oh, um…" Well, this was awful. He was asking her out, which was exactly what she wanted. But she was trying to avoid restaurants because she couldn't seem to resist the temptation to overeat. Maybe just this once? But she didn't want to go out with Joseph only once.

"It's okay," he said. "You can say no."

"You look disappointed."

"Naturally."

"I did not mean to say that out loud," Emily said. Her clumsy streak was particularly annoying when it affected her mouth. She was just so frazzled by the interest he showed in her. She wanted to take off her coat, and it was already off. "I don't want to say no."

"Just pretend I didn't ask then."

"No, I…" Emily decided to meet his honesty with her own. "I'd like to keep talking, but I always eat too much at restaurants."

"Oh." He smiled. "So you might be willing if I told you I meant we should eat here?"

"Uh…" She looked suspiciously at the soon-to-be-leftover candy.

"The chicken dinner in the cafeteria," he said. "They serve reasonable portions. And vegetables."

"That sounds good."

"The vegetables talked you into it?"

"That helped," she said, and smiled to herself. He didn't need to know she wanted to keep talking even if it meant going to a restaurant to watch him eat.

8

Joseph kept sneaking glances at Emily while they wrapped up the fishing poles and took down the cardboard pond. He still couldn't believe she'd come back to talk to him without him even asking. He had a faint worry that she would change her mind about extending their time and disappear while he was helping with the cleanup.

Of course, a more concrete worry was that his dad was helping with the chicken dinners. He might try to join their conversation. Joseph didn't think he'd say anything that was particularly worrisome. He'd just be in the way.

Emily did not disappear. Joseph's dad was serving chicken, not milling about the cafeteria. He didn't seem to notice that Joseph and Emily were together as they came through the line. Emily figured out the connection though. Joseph led her to an empty table in a corner. As they sat down, she said, "Was that your dad in the serving line?"

"Yes."

"He looks a lot like Isaac," she said.

Joseph cringed a little on the inside. Here it came, another joke about who the real twins were.

"Also," she smiled knowingly, "he greeted you like you knew each other."

"You didn't think a stranger would remind me to eat the green beans?"

Her smile was uncertain. "That's not what you thought I was going to say, was it?"

"No, I thought you were going to say something about how it's weird that Isaac looks more like our dad than me."

"I know Ruth is a redhead," Emily said. "Does your mom have red hair, too?"

He nodded. "And Adam."

"Oh, you have *two* brothers and a sister. You're the only one with dark hair?"

"Yeah."

"It bothers you to be the oddball?"

"No."

She looked confused. "But it bothers you that Isaac looks more like your dad than you do?"

"No."

"I don't get it," she said. "Why were you afraid I was going to comment on it?"

"I should have given you more credit." He really should have. Emily wasn't that predictable. "I thought you might be the five thousandth person to try to make a joke about twins who don't look alike when it's called fraternal."

Emily's eyes moved in a circle, like wheels literally turning in her head. "You and Isaac are twins?"

"You didn't know that?"

"I'm new here, remember?"

He remembered. Her arrival was memorable.

"I knew you were brothers, or I figured that out last Friday at least. I think I assumed Isaac was older. Probably because he's married and about to be a dad. But responsibility doesn't always correlate to age and... not that you seem irresponsible or... Sometimes I need to not open my mouth." Emily stuffed a large bite of chicken in her mouth in an apparent attempt to keep herself from talking more.

Joseph was amused by the occasional babbling though. It made Emily seem honest, as though she said what she actually thought instead of pausing to decide what he might want to hear. "Don't worry," he said. "I know what you mean. Isaac is sort of ahead of me in milestones. And he is technically older."

She smiled around the mouthful.

"Did you ever have a meal like this at your old church?"

"You mean a fundraiser or chicken specifically?" She eyed him like it was a strange question.

Maybe it was, but Joseph wanted to get her talking about herself again. He was grasping for a segue. "Either one," he said.

"Well..." She poked around her plate with her plastic fork. "The Knights of Columbus had fish fries during Lent. I went to a couple of those with my parents. What I remember about the last one is that it seemed like everyone else was either families with young kids or older people. I felt a little out of place. It was mostly the same demographics on Sundays. I was really excited to see that St. Jude's had a young adult group."

"There aren't many of us," Joseph said.

"Still... it sucks that I won't be able to go anymore."

"What?" He was shocked to hear this news since it was his fallback for when he'd get to see Emily next.

"It's sort of good, actually. Or the reason is. Because I was really not looking forward to another week. Though I feel bad about not going anymore."

She didn't want to go to another meeting but was disappointed to miss it? Joseph tried to figure out how to ask her to clarify without telling her that she didn't make any sense. "Why can't you come on Fridays anymore?"

"Because I got a new job." She grinned eagerly.

"Oh! That is good," he said. "Where?"

"I got hired at Burger Brothers just yesterday."

"Congratulations!" He'd always thought Chip and Paula were the kind of fun that was best in small doses. He hoped for Emily's sake that either he was wrong or she disagreed.

"I'm not sure I did the right thing," Emily said. "I mean about my old job. I was excited about being hired at Burger Brothers so I sent my now old boss an email about how I'd have to put in notice on Monday and then I realized it was weird to basically give notice about giving notice. But I've never really quit a job before." She paused for a bite but chewed fast as she had more to say. "At least a job I didn't like. I had a few summer jobs that I sort of quit just by telling someone when school started. My parents knew I was looking and... So anyway my old boss replied that I didn't need to bother coming in on Monday." Emily shrugged. "I think she was kind of upset with me, but it's done now."

"So are you starting the new job right away?"

Emily nodded, swallowed, and said, "Tuesday. This chicken is really good. I'm noticing after a few weeks on my own that I'm not a very creative cook. Most of what I've been eating is sort of bland and recipes seem to always be for at least four people. Is this vinegar or... Whatever it is is delicious." She popped another bite into her mouth.

Joseph was glad she was enjoying the meal he suggested. But she seemed to have completely forgotten that she was telling him about her new job, which may or may not have been connected to the Friday night group and her attendance at it. There weren't any topics he didn't want to hear about. He just wanted to make sure they eventually got back to discussing the next time he might see her.

Could he keep a mental path back if they kept talking about food? It probably didn't matter. He wasn't going to forget to ask about seeing her again. And if she was going to give bad news on that score, he'd just as soon wait until later. "What is your favorite food?" Joseph asked.

Emily appeared thoughtful. She put down her fork and turned to him with a very serious expression as she said, "Don't laugh."

Which naturally made Joseph want to laugh. He barely snickered before he got the impulse under control. "Sorry," he said. "Do you know how hard it is not to laugh when someone tells you not to laugh while looking like she's about to reveal something terribly funny."

"I know," Emily said. "Now that you got the laugh out of the way I can tell you that right now my favorite food might be Frosted Mini-Wheats."

"The cereal?"

"You've heard of it?" she asked sarcastically.

"What makes you say that's your favorite food?"

She raised her eyebrows and dipped her chin, looking very much as though she was about to give him a hard time about something. Possibly the definition of favorite. Then her face relaxed and she said, "Wait. You actually want to hear about it, don't you? You're not just going for friendly chitchat?"

"If there's a story, I want to hear it."

"Okay." Emily put her fork down and tucked some hair behind her ear. "The first week or so that I worked at the dentist office, I brought a lunch and stuck it in the refrigerator in the break room. A couple of times, it seemed as though it got moved around, like inside the bag moved around. I always put the sandwich, if there was one, on top so it wouldn't get squished and it was sort of on the side. And it seemed like the yogurt was…" She was moving her hands around as she talked to illustrate the moving lunch. It wasn't helping with a mental picture, but Joseph enjoyed the animation nonetheless.

She sighed as she seemed to give up on making her hands look like a cup of yogurt. "Anyway, I kept trying to convince myself it was my imagination… until I couldn't. Nothing was ever missing, but it freaked me out to think that someone was rifling through my lunch. I still don't know who it was. No one else ever mentioned anything weird like that. I just decided to start bringing lunches that didn't need to be refrigerated and keep it with me in my bag.

"One day I was about to leave, and I realized I hadn't packed anything to eat. I usually did it the night before because I'm too scattered in the morning. The first thing that popped into my head for a quick lunch was that I'd just opened the family size box of Mini-Wheats for breakfast that I bought because it was on sale and I knew it was going to take me forever to eat it and I didn't want to have it for breakfast *every* day so I poured some into a sandwich bag for lunch."

"Hang on," Joseph interrupted. "You didn't want to eat it for breakfast every day so you decided to eat it for breakfast *and* lunch?"

Emily smiled. Rather than being annoyed at being interrupted, she actually looked pleased that he was paying enough attention to have picked up on the flawed logic. "Well," she said, "I was thinking that eating it dry would be different than eating it with milk. Not that I'd be eating it twice in one day. My brain is not a morning person."

"Ha." He could laugh because it didn't sound as though she was berating herself, just comfortable enough to state the facts. "I'm guessing you discovered you like it without milk."

"Have you tried it?" she asked.

He shook his head. He couldn't honestly say that cereal had made it into his rotation.

"It's so good." Emily cast her eyes to the ceiling in what looked like a quick prayer of thanksgiving for the person who invented Mini-Wheats. "I've been eating it for lunch a few times a week since. Just stick a banana or some kind of fruit cup with it and my lunch is packed. A couple of times I ate it on the weekends and I still had to put some in a sandwich bag because if I ate it from the box I knew I'd keep going until the box was empty."

"You're not worried about getting sick of it?"

She shrugged at him. "There are several flavors. And I can always pick a new favorite food."

"A little bag of cereal and a banana?" Joseph said. "That's your whole lunch?"

"I didn't say it was a little bag." She gave him a cheeky grin, then seemed to remember the good food in front of her. She picked up her fork and poked Joseph's arm with the handle. "Besides, you're twice as big as I am. Of course you need to eat more."

At first, he wanted to protest the comparison to make sure she wasn't exaggerating because she was threatened by the size difference. But Emily didn't look as though she felt threatened. In fact, she glanced back at the muscle she'd poked as though she was impressed. That made his chest swell just a bit more. He still had to protest the suggestion because he was the shortest guy in his family and probably only had four or five inches on her. And as far as weight went...

She suddenly narrowed her eyes at him as though she knew he was trying to calculate the difference in their weights and was warning him against it. Then she smiled and said, "You're right," though he hadn't said anything. "Let's just say bigger."

"Fair enough," he said with a nod. He hadn't meant to criticize the amount of food she ate anyway. "Do you change your favorite food often?"

"I like a lot of things," she said. "When someone asks my favorite, I usually say the first like that comes to mind. And I know what you're thinking," she quickly added.

Joseph doubted that because he wasn't thinking anything.

"That doesn't mean I'm flighty," she said. "It only means I know what matters. When most people ask about my favorite book or song or whatever, they're just looking for some common ground to talk about. They're not asking me to choose which song of all the songs I know would I choose to listen to if I could only ever listen to one song. That would require serious thought. Keeping a conversation going should not require serious thought. Unless it's…um…"

"An important conversation?" Joseph tried.

"Sort of. Yeah." Emily started to nod but paused. "Well… they're two different things. There are important conversations, ones that involve decisions and consequences, and… those don't involve naming your favorite anything. The word favorite sort of implies trivial… triviality."

Joseph almost laughed. He agreed completely with what she said. He was amused by the paradox of how much thought she seemed to have given to declaring something unimportant.

"Are you trying not to laugh at me?" she asked.

That helped him straighten his face. "I think you make a good point."

"I think you did not answer my question."

"I was not laughing at you," he said. "I was entertained by the way you talked about triviality with conviction."

She took a bite while she considered it, which pulled all his attention to her mouth and distracted him with the temptation there. "I suppose that's a little funny," she conceded.

Joseph returned his mind to the conversation as she graced

him with a lovely smile. Unfortunately, her eyes quickly revealed that the smile wasn't for him at all. She was looking past him to where Isaac was approaching.

"Hi," she said brightly. To Isaac. The interloper.

Isaac gave a brief nod to his brother before he addressed Emily. "Hello. How are you enjoying the festival?"

"It's great." She pointed to her almost empty plate. "The chicken is awesome."

"I'll tell Dad you like it," Isaac said. "He actually sent me over here to check on you guys. Do you need anything?"

Emily shook her head.

The only thing Joseph needed was for Isaac to go away.

But Isaac kept talking. "Yeah, he pointed out how the two of you were sitting way over here in the corner, almost like you wanted to be alone. I was like, I should definitely go over there and make sure everything's okay." He pulled out a chair and sat down across from them as he finished talking.

Joseph made a mental note to invite his brother over to spar on those new mats. He glanced sideways at Emily. She didn't appear embarrassed by the insinuation. Either she sensed Joseph's intentions and was fine with that or had no intentions of her own and didn't think there was anything to be embarrassed about.

"I was just thinking," Emily said. She looked between the brothers, happy to include them both in the conversation. "I remember a time I helped with something sort of like this. We didn't have a regular fall festival or anything at my church. It was... I think it was a veterans' lunch, so probably Veterans Day or Memorial Day. Anyway, my whole class helped. I was assigned to filling drinks. But I wasn't allowed to pour the coffee because it was hot. I must have been eleven or twelve and I was so indignant that they didn't think I could handle coffee. I was like I'm not a toddler. Why does everyone think I'm going to burn myself?"

Emily laughed at her past reaction. "Now I know they weren't worried about me burning myself so much as someone else. I was a klutzy kid. We're all lucky I didn't pour lemonade in anyone's lap."

Joseph gave her a teasing look. "Are you going to be pouring drinks at Burger Brothers?"

"No." She threw an elbow at his ribs. "People get their own drinks, which I think you know. And I'm a little better now."

"Are you working at Burger Brothers?" Isaac asked.

Emily nodded eagerly. "I start on Tuesday."

"Cool," Isaac said. "You were just complaining about your old job. That was a quick change."

"It was." She sucked in a nervous breath. "I hope I still feel as blessed as I do now after I start the job."

"I think it'll work out," Joseph said.

Isaac agreed. "You seem to be going into it with a good attitude and that always helps."

It was clear Emily was looking forward to the new job. Her eyes glittered when she thought of it, and Joseph could picture her dancing on the inside. Then, because of Paula, he pictured her gliding instead. "Hey," he said. "Are you gonna wear skates?"

Her mouth fell open at the question. Panic covered her face. "I didn't think to ask that," she said. "Are other employees expected to... I can't skate."

"Relax." Isaac laid a hand on the table in front of her. "I've never seen anyone besides Paula skating. I think that's just her thing."

"Yeah, I was kidding," Joseph added. "I just thought it was a funny idea."

"It's not funny," she said, still sounding as though her heart was racing. "I would be falling all over the place."

"Until you got good at it," Joseph said.

Emily sighed again. "I'd either break my leg or get fired first. Maybe both."

Isaac raised himself from his chair. "Well, if you're done I can clear your places for you."

Joseph quickly pushed his empty plate at his brother.

Emily pushed hers more slowly. "Are you sure?"

"That's what I'm here for."

"Oh, you're a volunteer?" she said.

"Of course." Isaac winked. "No one says no to Mrs. Donnelly. But sometimes they conveniently forget that they didn't say no."

Emily smiled and said, "Thanks," as he picked up her plate.

"I'll see you on Friday then?"

"Actually, you won't." Emily's smile dropped off her face. "I can't come on Fridays anymore."

Isaac had been about to walk away. He turned back and set the plates on the table. "Why not?"

"I'll be working until eight now. With the meetings only going until 8:30 there's no point in me showing up just in time to disrupt the end."

"Oh, that's too bad." Isaac sounded disappointed.

Joseph wasn't disappointed. He refused to be disappointed because there had to be a way to fix the situation. "What if we changed the time?" he asked.

"The time the young adult group meets?" Emily sounded mystified. The idea certainly hadn't occurred to her.

There was enough hope in her eyes that Joseph pressed ahead. "Sure," he said. He gestured to Isaac. "Half the regulars are family. We can convince them to change."

"Well..." Isaac began to nod slowly. "Yeah. If we bumped it

back an hour, you'd only be a few minutes late. That'd be fine. Trust me, no one would mind if you come smelling like hamburgers. In fact, you can sit by me."

Emily laughed.

"And we're all kind of young," Joseph said. "Surely we can stay up to the wee hours of 9:30."

Now Isaac laughed. "You're the one who's missed half the meetings because they were past your bedtime."

"I also have a new job," Joseph reminded his brother. "And a new bedtime. Starting in a few days anyway."

"You have a new job?" Emily looked very curious.

But Joseph didn't want to derail the planning. "I do," he acknowledged quickly. "We need to work this out though."

"Nothing to work out," Isaac said. "We'll just have Ruth and Gabriel announce the new start time next week – sorry you'll have to miss one – and put it in the bulletin. Then the week after that we'll start at eight and everybody's happy."

"Just like that?" Emily asked.

"Yeah." Isaac picked up the plates again. "We can still talk Baby Ruth into anything."

"As long as we don't call her Baby Ruth," Joseph said.

"And Gabriel will go along with whatever she wants because…" Isaac grinned broadly and in Joseph's opinion stupidly. "Well, for the same reason I do what Jessica wants and the same reason that Joseph… See you a week from Friday, Emily." He turned away with the plates as she waved.

He'd left the cups even though Joseph's was empty.

Emily had only a sip of water left, which she quickly downed. She looked at the table uncertainly. She seemed to be thinking the same thing Joseph was. They were done. Their time had come to an end unless someone made a suggestion otherwise.

Suddenly, Joseph was nervous. The kind of nervous that made his stomach put a vice grip on the meal he'd just eaten. Asking her to join him for that meal was hard enough, and that could've been perceived as a friendly gesture after she'd kept him company in the fishing game. He was about to venture into unambiguous I want to date you territory where he could get an equally unambiguous rejection.

"I'd like to hear about that new job sometime," Emily said first.

She was going to make it that easy? Oh, this was a woman he could love. "Yes," he said, "we should arrange a time for me to bore you with lots of details."

She nodded expectantly.

"Uh… I'm thinking about our schedules. I have three more shifts to drive. Monday, Wednesday and Thursday. It sounds like you'll be working whenever I'm awake and not working." Except for Monday afternoon. He had to fight himself not to suggest a time less than twenty-four hours away. Too aggressive might come across poorly. "How about Saturday?" he asked.

"Okay."

"Okay?" He was shockingly relieved considering that Emily was the one who initiated the negotiation.

"I don't think…" She paused to think. "I don't think I have anything at all planned for Saturday."

Joseph nodded happily. This would be perfect if only he could think of a suggestion of what to do. He didn't want to propose the obvious dinner. Besides her reluctance to eat out, a meal would only give them an hour or so together. He wanted to suggest something longer. But the frigid weather of November was a problem. It pretty much ruled out anything outdoors. The only indoor things that popped into his head – movies and bowling – were loud and not great for real conversations.

"Could you… show me?" Emily asked tentatively.

"Show you what?"

"I'm taking a guess that your new job has something to do with the building covered in paper," she said. "I know you said it was a surprise and if it's a dangerous construction site then… But maybe if it's… Are you willing to show me the inside?"

"Yes." That wasn't just an idea, it was a great idea. Joseph got excited about sharing his hopes and plans with Emily in the space she could visualize them. "Come knock on the door after lunch, and I'll let you in. About what time would that be?"

"I guess around 1 o'clock. Maybe 1:30?"

"One sounds perfect," he said.

She smiled at what he hoped sounded eager and not demanding. When she got up to leave, she mumbled something. She was bent over to collect her bag so he didn't hear well, but it sounded like, "No vegetables needed."

It took him a moment, but if he interpreted right, it was a good sign. He watched her walk out the door thinking that Saturday was not going to arrive fast enough.

9

By Friday, Emily was beginning to feel as though she knew what she was doing at her new job. The first day had been almost all cleaning. She washed a few things in the kitchen but mostly wiped down table after table after table. And benches and chairs, too. Chip instructed her to never clean a table without also cleaning where people sit. No one wanted to sit in someone else's crumbs and nothing ruined a day like sitting in a blob of ketchup. This wasn't the overkill Emily first assumed. People could be surprisingly messy.

The second day she got to chop onions and slice tomatoes, which was more difficult than she expected. She had to be shown several times how to slice the tomatoes without squeezing them into weird shapes, and she still couldn't do it. Chip held them so gently with his bigger and stronger hands. It frustrated her not to be able to do the same.

She kept working on it while the tomatoes she had "strangled" were chopped further to put in salads. When Chip nodded approval at her first salad and left her to make a few on her own, Emily felt as though she'd successfully split an atom. She'd hummed a little as she made those salads and talked to them like dear friends.

Luke did not approve of talking to salads. He was a coworker and Chip's nephew. She guessed he was in his early thirties. He was the bearded guy she'd seen take over the register when Chip interviewed her. Emily hadn't figured out what his deal was yet, but he spent a lot of time brooding or sighing darkly before walking away from a conversation. Or a slightly crazy person talking to lettuce.

Near the end of the third day, Thursday, Emily actually got to take a few orders. She had trouble doing it with a straight face. The register was really old. Chip called it Beethoven. He explained how to use it in his gruff way. There were buttons for the most common menu items and the things most often asked to be added or left off.

The button used to modify an order had the word modify printed on it. Chip called it the "someone's being difficult" button, and that was what gave Emily trouble. When someone asked for no mustard, she heard Chip's tired voice telling her someone was being difficult. She hoped she managed to present the escaping giggles as trying to act super friendly.

She came in on Friday and was introduced to the fryer. Chip said, "Dump, submerge, timer." Then he demonstrated. Though the timer was different than the place she'd worked before college, the process was familiar so there was at least one thing she could catch on to quickly. Chip had told her she would need to be there several weeks before he trusted her on the grill and that she should watch as much as possible in the meantime. He took the burgers seriously. That was her primary observation so far. The man was not to be interrupted when he had anything sizzling.

He assigned her to run Beethoven during the lunch rush. Emily knew she wasn't going fast enough, but people seemed to recognize her as new and were generally patient. It was one benefit of a small town. Seeing two friendly faces helped her to relax as Ruth and Ella stepped up to order.

"Hi, Emily," Ruth said.

Ella smiled and nodded a greeting.

"Hello," she said. "Welcome to Burger Brothers."

"How do you like it here?" Ruth asked.

Emily nodded. "So far, so good."

"Great. We'll have two standard cheeseburgers. To go."

"Okay." Emily pushed a standard cheeseburger and glanced at the modify button. "You don't want to be difficult?" Then she kicked herself for saying that out loud. Perhaps she was too relaxed.

But Ruth just laughed and said, "You sound like Chip already."

The man in question cleared his throat loudly behind her. He was keeping a sharp ear open for any trouble she might have.

Emily winced apologetically at Ruth and Ella before she told them the total in her most professional voice.

"The new time for Friday will run in this week's bulletin," Ruth said. "So we'll see you next week?"

"Yeah. Thank you so much for changing it for me."

"It's no big deal." Ruth tucked her card back into her purse as she spoke. "And Isaac pointed out that Sebastian's been late a few times. If he's having trouble getting there at seven, the new time could work out for a lot of people."

"I hope so."

The two women moved aside. The next person in line was a man in a police uniform. A desire to be on her best behavior surged through Emily, as though the man might arrest her if she wasn't polite enough.

Before she could say a word, Chip growled, "Do *not* let him order a veggie burger."

Emily gulped and smiled at the policeman.

He returned the smile. With a nod towards Chip, who he had evidently heard, he said, "I will have a veggie patty, please. With a large Coke."

Chip said nothing. She entered the order tentatively, not sure if he might actually bite this time.

The rumble of skates indicated that Paula was fast

approaching. She grabbed the counter at Emily's elbow to stop herself as she nodded to the policeman. "Howdy, Ryan."

"Paula." He nodded back. "How are you today?"

"Still rolling," she said. Then she tipped her head towards Emily with a stage whisper. "Don't worry, honey, they argue about the name every time."

"There's no argument," Chip said, "because it's my menu."

Ryan the police officer laughed as he took his cup and receipt. "A place called Burger Brothers can't serve patties."

Chip only grunted, which might have actually been covering a laugh.

"And tell your husband I want to see some grill lines this time," Ryan added.

There was no one else in line so Emily stepped back to let him chat with Paula while she watched Chip in action. Luke was there, too, wrapping up the burgers for Ruth and Ella. She waved to them as they took their lunch and left.

That veggie burger or patty or whatever – Emily was afraid she would have trouble remembering what she was supposed to call it – was pretty thoroughly blackened when Chip was done with it. That seemed like a bad way to treat a customer. But the policeman apparently kept coming back so she guessed Chip knew what he was doing.

She took a few more orders before things settled down for the afternoon. Paula went home as the high school kids began to arrive. Burger Brothers was a popular after school hangout, despite the fact that many of the kids appeared afraid of or at least intimidated by Chip and Luke. A few of the kids were there to work. They passed baskets of fries and an occasional burger through the window to their peers, who cast furtive glances into the kitchen.

Emily had already learned that there was a calm time between four and five where she could eat an early dinner. If she didn't take advantage, she would need to wait until she got home after eight. She didn't like to eat late in the evenings so she intended to eat early. But there was a problem.

"Oh, nuts!" she said as she pushed her bag back under the counter.

Luke sent a questioning look her way.

"I forgot my dinner," Emily said.

He rolled his eyes. "You mean the breakfast you eat at odd times?"

She'd actually brought a sandwich for a meal once, but defending her affinity for Mini-Wheats wasn't the point. "Yes," she said.

"You do know that free food is a perk of the job?"

Chip raised an eyebrow at Emily, daring her not to jump up and down at the prospect of eating his food.

"I... uh... the burgers are just kind of big. I'm trying not to overeat."

Luke sighed and refocused on the cutting board he was cleaning.

Chip glared at her as though she'd insulted his mother. But at the same time, he picked up a spatula and chopped a burger in half before he flipped it onto the grill. He waved her closer and said, "Lesson one. All burgers are either done or well done."

She nodded seriously.

"Don't touch it while it's cooking," he said as he nudged it to the side with his spatula.

Emily didn't understand if nudges didn't count as touching or if he was stating the obvious. "With my fingers?" she asked.

He grunted, shook his head, then looked at her rather sadly. "You are not ready."

Apparently not. She watched in silence as he poked the burger around on the grill, flipping it twice, before he handed it to her on a plate. She was allowed to finish it herself. She wrapped it in half a bun with mustard, ketchup and a whole slice of cheese. It was so delicious. This place was going to be even more tempting from now on.

Luke had made himself a full burger and assigned the teenagers to some other cleaning. There were two chairs behind the counter between the order window and the pickup window. Emily sat in one of them. Luke sat in the other. Chip stood at the window watching the loud but generally well-behaved mob.

"You know Ruth Ziebert?" Luke asked suddenly.

"A little," Emily said. Though she smiled at the mention of Ruth because it immediately made her think of Ruth's brother, the one she was looking forward to seeing the next day.

"She said something about Friday when she was here," Luke said. "Is that the thing at St. Jude's?"

"Yeah, that's how I know her. Do you, um..." Emily hesitated, trying to keep from tripping over her own tongue as she often did. She'd started to ask if he knew Ruth was dating Gabriel, which might imply a motive for bringing her up. Then she was going to ask if he knew Ruth's bothers. That would also be too personal. "Do you go to St. Jude's?" she asked. Then she gave herself a mental slap for landing on religion when trying to keep a conversation casual.

Luke only shrugged and said, "Sometimes."

"And the Friday night meetings?" In for a penny...

"I was just there once."

"They're changing the time from seven to eight," Emily said. "Just in case it's the time that made you not go more."

He sighed. It was a sigh of annoyance.

Emily stuffed the last bite of her dinner into her mouth and chewed slowly to keep from saying anything else annoying. No wonder people came back even when Chip was crabby. It was so good she wanted more, and not because she was hungry. Her willpower would either crumble or become cast iron.

Oddly, Luke didn't seem to be done with the conversation that was bothering him. "You go on Fridays?" he asked.

"Uh… not tonight because the new time starts next week. I've been to the last few though."

"Who else?"

"Who else attends the meetings?" Emily asked. It sounded like a simple question, but Luke asked as though he was expecting an answer that was very wrong.

He grunted at her request for clarification.

"Well, there's Ruth of course and Gabriel. I met his brother last week. Eric. And Ruth's brother Isaac with his wife. Joseph was there last week as well." Did she manage to say his name as though it was simply part of the list? Emily kept going anyway. "Also Ella and Julia and Sebastian, and I think I'm forgetting someone…"

She looked at Luke when she gave up thinking of any other names. He was clearly disgruntled about something. It occurred to her that all the people she mentioned were younger than he was. Maybe he was wondering if he still qualified as a young adult.

"I'm sure you'd be more than welcome," she said. She was about to ask if the time change would make it more convenient, but he was already shaking his head. She held her tongue.

He stood up with his plate and a very dark look on his face. "I'm afraid I can't associate with people who include the likes of Sebastian Jones."

Emily was taken aback by the tone that suggested someone who seemed perfectly nice might actually be pure evil.

"Make sure you stay away from him," Luke said. "My sister is married to a guy like that."

"Like what?" The question slipped out more argumentative than she intended. But a guy she barely knew couldn't just issue a warning with no explanation whatsoever.

Apparently, he thought he could because he walked away without another word. Emily glanced at Chip. He was watching his nephew's back with sad eyes. There was a story there, and it didn't feel like the right time to ask. Emily stepped to the register. She saw a family with young children entering and turned to Chip to see if she should take their order.

He nodded and even smiled faintly. It might have been the first time he'd smiled at her all week. Somehow, it made her realize how happy he looked when he was scowling at everyone. The kids made her push the someone's being difficult button so many times that Emily was smiling brightly by the time the order was entered and Chip was back to normal.

After a busy evening, she went home to wonder if her parents had forgotten how to tell time. She'd missed calls from both of them in the last hour, and they knew what time she got off work. She kicked off her shoes and got comfortable on the couch before she called her dad. His call was more recent, and she knew she'd end up talking to both parents no matter which number she dialed.

"Emily! Good to hear from you." He said it like they hadn't spoken for months rather than days.

"Hi, Dad."

"Tell me you had something more substantial than cereal today."

"I actually had a cheeseburger for dinner."

"Was it as good as before?"

"Better." She laughed to herself to think that her doctor father seemed to be celebrating a cheeseburger as a healthy choice.

"Glad to hear it," he said. "Your mother worries about you wasting away."

"Why do I feel like I need to explain to you that quantity matters?" She pictured her measured bag of cereal. "If I was eating an entire box of cereal at every meal, I certainly wouldn't be in danger of wasting away."

"I saw the cutest toddler today."

Emily rolled with the abrupt subject change. "Aren't most toddlers cute, Dad?"

"This one was at that age where they want a name for everything," he said. "She just kept pointing and saying 'this' at everything around her."

"That is cute," Emily agreed. She pictured a small boy with dark curly hair and blue eyes, someone who looked like Joseph in miniature but with something of herself in the shape of his eyes. Was the picture a message from God that her life was finally moving forward in a good direction? Or was it simply a result of her new infatuation?

"Emily?"

"Oh. Yeah?" The picture was distracting no matter where it came from.

"I asked if you were ready to come back to the office yet?" he said. "Are you thinking about it?"

"No." Best not to get his hopes up when she was actually thinking of something very different. Emily had always assumed she would have a job and a family. Now talking about a job had her head filling with thoughts of children. Not children popping in and out of a doctor's office, but children in her home. Children asking her where things were and arguing over whose turn it was to do something. It was a picture where her family was her job. Was she allowed to want that? Wasn't a modern woman supposed to have it all and want it all? Emily didn't know where all the crazy ideas were coming from so she shook them off to focus on her existing family.

"Dad, I think I'm going to like this job at Burger Brothers. At least for now."

"I suppose there's less chance of you starving yourself working near food."

"I'm not starving myself, Dad. But I am two pounds closer to my goal."

He made a noise of displeasure, then said something Emily couldn't hear. There was also a female voice in the background, her mom no doubt. When her dad returned to the phone, he said, "What happens when you reach your goal weight?"

"I'm not sure," she said. "The point is to eat a diet that's… doesn't feel like a diet. I guess I'm just assuming I'll level out around my college weight." Emily sort of shrugged to herself. She wouldn't mind being a few points either side of her goal. What she did mind was the idea that she probably wouldn't know she'd reached that plateau until she'd been there for a while.

"You won't just make a new goal?" her dad asked.

"What?"

"That's how these things work," he said. "The first goal isn't enough, then the second. You need to be satisfied with the way you look. And you are beautiful."

"So by these things, you mean eating disorders. I don't have an eating disorder."

"Your mother worries about… She wants to talk to you herself. Goodnight, honey."

"Night, Dad."

Emily knew it was only a matter of time before her mom took the phone as soon as she heard her in the background. And she knew what her mom wanted to talk about. It wasn't a surprise when she didn't even say hello before she said, "So you're seeing Joseph tomorrow?"

"That's still the plan."

"Have you talked to him since Sunday?"

"No." Emily could hear the wistfulness in her own voice.

"Why not?"

"I told you I didn't get his number."

A loud sigh came through the phone. "But you have his sister's."

Emily had been regretting that thought almost as much as letting it slip out of her mouth. The last time she'd spoken to her mom – Tuesday after her first day of work – she'd talked a lot about the time she'd spent with Joseph and the plans they'd made for Saturday. She'd also mentioned that she'd neglected to get his phone number. Then, just because the thought happened to pop into her head, she'd said she could get the number from Ruth if anything came up.

Emily's mom had tried to convince her to get his number right away to chat. She'd said that guys needed encouragement and that showing some interest right away would help move things along. Emily had been thinking about it ever since. She didn't want to be pushy and wasn't concerned with moving things along. But she did want to talk to him. Getting the number from Ruth should not have been a big deal. Unfortunately, Emily thought about it too much for it to stay a small deal.

"Well, it's too late now," she said to her mom.

"Make sure you get his number tomorrow."

Emily felt her eyes rolling. "If I don't end up with his number, it means things went badly enough that I won't need it."

"Don't say that," her mom admonished. "Think positively. Joseph could be my key to grandchildren."

"No offense, Mom, but I plan to *not* tell him that." Although as she said it, Emily realized that she'd already hinted as much when she was telling Joseph about her mom's pressure for grandkids. Plus, she was always saying things she hadn't planned to say.

"Did you at least ask him if he wants kids?"

"At least?" Emily thought again about how much time they'd spent talking about her. When she started asking about him, whether or not he wanted kids probably shouldn't be the least of the questions. She spent the next few minutes on the phone listening to all the other things her mom thought she should find out.

10

She could be there in a few minutes. Joseph stared at the last text from his mom. She'd suggested a few times in the last week that she was ready to see his "new" place. Always with the insinuation-laced quotation marks. He'd been able to put her off because of work. Now it was Saturday, and he had no job.

Emily wasn't coming over until 1 o'clock. That gave him about three free hours. He'd admitted as much to his mom but hadn't exactly meant it as an invitation. Of course, if he showed her around now, he could get the tour over with and distract himself at the same time. Watching the clock until Emily got there didn't sound any more fun than making his mom annoyed with him.

He told his mom she could come on over. Her reply was only an exclamation point. Joseph sighed at the enthusiasm he sensed in the single character and went downstairs to unlock the front door. When his mom said a few minutes, she meant a few minutes. In fact, he had barely begun to contemplate his unpainted walls – one decision giving him an inordinate amount of trouble – when he caught sight of her car through a crack in the paper on the window.

Joseph jogged over to flip the lights on. He was used to working with only the back light but thought the space should look as nice as possible for a tour. Though maybe he'd be better off not highlighting the unfinished parts when Emily was there. For his mom, he planned to point out those unfinished bits to reinforce that he had not waited until the last possible second to tell her about it.

She knocked lightly on the front door. Joseph stood back as he opened it wide and swept an arm towards what would soon be The Family Gym. He'd thought for a long time about a more imaginative name. But every time he'd asked himself what to call his family gym... Well, it seemed obvious even if it wasn't inspired.

Joanna Ziebert scanned the large room before her eyes settled on her son, who prepared himself for a barrage of questions about the place. She said, "There's a girl, too?"

"Um..." That was not among the questions Joseph had expected. He glanced around the room even though he knew there was no one else around.

"A girl," she repeated, pulling her hands sternly to her hips. "Your father informs me that there is a girl in your life."

"Oh." That girl. Emily. His dad had seen him with Emily at the festival.

"Wipe that smile off your face and tell me how long you've been seeing her without telling your mother. When did you become the secretive type?"

"I'm not," he said. "I... There isn't anything to tell regarding Emily. Not yet. This is sort of our first date."

"This?" She looked around as though she, too, was expecting to find a previously unnoticed third person.

"She's coming over later."

"For dinner?"

"No."

"Lunch?" She looked at her watch hopefully.

"No, sort of in between those."

"In between?" His mom drew her mouth back in a wince. "I know you love to be... frugal, honey. But I'm not sure it's a good idea to try to date without spending money."

Joseph laughed because he *was* very careful with money and because this was one time he hadn't thought about it. "I'm not trying to be cheap by not feeding her, Mom. It was her idea to get together when we could just talk. I think it's a good idea though because if we can have a conversation without food or anything to distract us, that's probably a good sign."

She nodded, but she said, "You should still have something to offer her, just in case. It's polite, you know, to offer food to guests."

He did have a plate of snacks, not out of politeness but from the very selfish hope that they'd be getting along so well neither of them would want her to leave at dinnertime. His mom didn't need to know that. "I'm not sure how polite that would be in this case," he said. "She might not want me to stick food in front of her because she's on a diet or something."

"Oh." She raised her eyebrows. "Does that say red flag to you?"

"Should it?"

"Not necessarily." Her eyebrows relaxed as she explained. "But take your aunt Rhonda for example. You know she's always talking about being on a diet but never pays any attention to what she eats. She only says she's dieting to get people to tell her she looks great the way she is. That's only the tip of her insecurities, which likely contributed to both her divorces and the failed relationships since."

Aunt Rhonda did spend a lot of energy fishing for compliments. It was kind of annoying. Joseph didn't think he'd picked up that vibe from Emily.

"And then there's this woman I work with," his mom continued. "She's about fifty pounds overweight and could probably benefit from dropping a few of them. It seems every other week she's starting a new diet." She paused for air quotes. "They all involve being able to eat as much as she wants as long as she avoids one specific thing. They're shortcuts. Shortcuts she gives up on almost immediately. You are not afraid of hard work so someone who is would be a poor match for you."

"Interesting," Joseph said. His instinct was to deflect, to act as though he was paying little attention to this lecture disguised as advice. He couldn't help listening though. As much as he insisted there was nothing to tell regarding Emily, he was already invested. It was smart to listen for traits his attraction might make him want to ignore. He thought of Emily making three cakes to follow through on her commitment to the cake walk when she could have simply bought one. That was a frivolous example, but it certainly didn't paint her as a person who looked for shortcuts or gave up easily.

His mother sighed and said, "Can I trust you to tell me when there is something to tell?"

"I thought you were here for a tour," he said.

She smiled and took off her coat, looking like someone who planned to stay for a lengthy tour.

"Coat hooks!" Joseph said.

His mom folded her coat over her arm as she squinted at his outburst.

She could walk around like that, but anyone engaging in real exercise would need a place to leave stuff. "I was just realizing I haven't planned a place for coat hooks."

"Right there." She pointed.

"You think?" he asked. It didn't seem as though she'd given it any consideration at all.

"You can't hang coats on the window," she said with a look of distaste. "They'd be in the way by the counter and the longer ones would drag on the floor. That wall is next closest to the door."

"I guess."

"What else do you need my help with?" She looked around eagerly.

Joseph enjoyed the enthusiasm as he began to show her the space and talk more about his plans for it. The tour went pretty well. She nodded a lot and the suggestions she offered were clearly that... suggestions. There was no indication she'd be offended if they weren't followed.

His mom's positive reactions faded as he took her up the back stairs to his apartment. Her eyes flickered around while the rest of her expression stayed eerily still, perhaps because there were so many criticisms she couldn't decide which was most important to voice.

Joseph decided to throw out some good points while she was speechless. "It's actually a little bigger than my old place. All these windows let in a lot of natural light. The location is convenient, too. I almost always walk to Seymour's."

"You walk to Seymour's?" Her question sounded rhetorical and like the beginning of a litany. "And then what? I don't see a kitchen."

It was true that there wasn't an obvious kitchen, but the basics were there. The space had been a big room with a bathroom in the back when he'd bought it. He walled off a bedroom around the bathroom and installed a sink and short countertop on the outside of that wall. He waved his mom in that direction. "There's a sink here and microwave over there. I can set a glass on that end table while I eat."

"The windows are... They seem drafty and the view of the alley is..." She paused but apparently couldn't think of an appropriately disapproving adjective. She simply said, "You have a view of the back alley."

The view wasn't pretty, but he didn't spend much time gazing out the windows. The gym had a high ceiling and the apartment only made a second floor above the restrooms and storage area so there were no windows along the front wall. "It's private," he said lamely.

His mom tore her eyes from the pile of garbage behind the next building. Or perhaps she'd been looking at the towels he'd stuffed along the window sill. She tried to don an encouraging smile. "What is your next step here?"

Joseph's next step was nothing. He considered the place livable and intended to focus only on the gym for the foreseeable future. But it seemed she would hold back her criticisms as long as the space was a work in progress. He hesitated to tell her that progress was stalled.

"Have you picked out some... uh... carpet?" She ran the toe of her shoe over glue marks where old flooring had been ripped up.

"Not yet," he said.

"You're going to put something down, right?" She unfolded her coat as she spoke and slipped her arms into it against the chill in the room.

Joseph had a sweatshirt and a bundle of nervous energy to keep him warm. "Yeah, carpet, eventually," he said. "I sort of planned for that to be last. Don't want to have to cover it to paint." He waved a hand at one of the other things that needed to be done eventually, hoping she wasn't going to ask for a time frame.

Her shoe continued to focus attention on the bare floor, which is why Joseph was a little confused when she said, "What about my grandchildren?"

"What?"

"Your plans used to include hope for a big family. How does this...?" She trailed off with a helpless gesture at the floor, as though a lot of things hinged on the nonexistent carpet.

"Are you suggesting I can't talk anyone into marrying me until this place is properly decorated?" He intended to sound sarcastic, but he heard a touch of concern in his own voice. It hadn't occurred to him that women other than his mom might disapprove of the state of his apartment. Did it say something about him that Emily wouldn't like?

His mom laughed, apparently unaware of any concern. "No good woman is concerned with window dressing, literal or figurative, when looking for a man. She might even be happy to have a say in the finishing touches someday." She swept her arm wide. "I meant there isn't room for a big family here. There's just one bedroom. Have you changed your mind or... I hope you haven't given up."

"No, I... I figure there's room for a wife and one or two babies. Those things aren't going to happen tomorrow or even... Hopefully, by the time I need more space, the gym will have been running for a couple years and I'll know whether or not it can support a family. I thought I might eventually rent this space out to help pay for a house."

She nodded. Then she sighed and shook her head. "You've always been smart with money. I'm not really worried, I just... This place is so clearly covering only the bare minimum for life it almost amuses me. Will you invite me to stay for lunch so I can see how functional your, uh, kitchen is?"

"I like the hesitation on calling it a kitchen, Mom."

"There really isn't a kitchen."

"Maybe not, but it works," Joseph said. "And I will show you." He thought for a moment about what to make that would prove he wasn't eating cold cereal for every meal. He cooked some eggs in the microwave and added slices of cheese and mayo to make sandwiches that his mom admitted were very good even though she rolled her eyes at having to eat standing over the counter. There was one chair, which he offered to her, but she preferred to eat standing up than with a plate on her lap.

"You used to have a table," she said.

"Yeah, I sold it when I moved."

She set her sandwich on her plate as she scrunched her nose. "That table was a hand-me-down from me and your dad. I know it wasn't in great shape so you couldn't have gotten much for it."

"I wasn't trying to make a profit," Joseph said. "There was a guy at work looking for a table. Apparently, one of his kids broke the leg off theirs when he was climbing on it. The guy had it duct-taped as a temporary fix and was trying to hit garage sales to luck into a replacement. I don't know if he couldn't afford a new one or just didn't want to spend that much, but at any rate I sold him mine for ten bucks."

"Yes." His mom nodded. "I remember now that you told me about it at the time. I guess I'd assumed you bought yourself a new table afterwards. Of course, I also assumed I knew where you lived."

Joseph stuffed a bite of egg sandwich in his mouth to prevent himself from commenting on the dig. He knew he was forgiven for the delay in sharing as much as he knew his mom wouldn't forget any time soon.

She helped him clean up after they ate, then suggested they return to the gym to hear more about his plans. She seemed interested in the classes he hoped to offer and thought the rotating artwork was a great idea. When she asked to see the equipment he'd bought for a second time though, he suspected she might be stalling until Emily arrived. It was an idea that might not have occurred to him if he hadn't already been preoccupied with that impending arrival.

"Why do you keep checking the time?" his mom asked.

He only shrugged. He would have admitted he was looking forward to seeing Emily if his mom's eyes had been less sparkly in their enjoyment.

"Are you thinking you don't have time to finish the tour you promised your mother?"

"No, I'm wondering why you want to see the storage room again."

"Well, I only got a cursory look the first time," she said, slowly, as though she was saying the words as she thought of them. "Now that you've been talking about the specific classes and… How many jump ropes do you have?"

He laughed as the stalling became even more obvious. "Do you really want to go back there and count jump ropes?"

"I'm happy to see whatever you want to show me."

"I already showed you the jump ropes."

"Are you trying to get rid of me?" she asked, wearing a look of fake sadness.

Joseph knew it was fake, but she pulled it off so well he still felt a small prick of guilt. "Did I say I was trying to get rid of you?"

"You didn't have to say it," she said. A flicker of a smile showed through her somber appearance. "You're trying to get rid of your own mother, the woman who gave you life, who had to get up eight times a night when you were an infant."

"Isaac gets half the blame for that so you're going to have to call him if you want to continue this guilt trip."

She dropped the act, then abruptly asked, "Have you talked to your brother lately?"

Joseph knew by the sudden shift in tone that she was not talking about Isaac. He shook his head. "I don't think I've talked to Adam since the last time we were both at your house."

She nodded. "I get brief texts now and then. Usually just a heads up that he's not able to make Sunday dinner."

"I think he feels like the black sheep of the family," Joseph said, remembering that people used to teasingly give him that title because of his dark hair in a family of redheads. "Maybe if they actually start planning a wedding, the family could get involved with that and... sort of start to build a relationship with Kayla."

The idea sounded pathetic before he'd even finished saying it, partly because no one expected Kayla and Adam to start planning a wedding and partly because it was difficult to picture Kayla involving his family in something like that. She didn't seem interested in improving the situation, which left Adam stuck in the middle. Joseph didn't blame his mom for looking skeptical. She didn't get a chance to respond with more than the doubtful expression before they were interrupted by a gentle rap at the front door.

They were near the center of the room. Joseph quickly jogged towards the door. His mom sounded nearly as excited as she said, "Now I get to meet her."

Joseph was so happy Emily was there that he didn't mind so much that his mom was also still there. He threw open the door and was nearly knocked over by her smile. She appeared delighted to see him, which was somehow both expected and shocking. "Hi," he said.

Her smile grew. "Hi."

Then her eyes drifted over his shoulder to where his mom was approaching the door at a slower pace. Joseph's satisfaction was dimmed to see that she appeared no less delighted. He didn't feel quite as special when he wasn't the only one to warrant that smile. Apparently, Emily just couldn't help looking radiant any more than Joseph could help forgetting manners.

A hand reached past him as another pushed him aside. "Hi, I'm Joseph's mom, Joanna Ziebert."

Emily took the extended hand as she introduced herself and was yanked through the doorway.

"Come in! Come in! Joseph's been giving me a little tour, but I know he's much more interested in showing you around the place."

Joseph nodded carefully. It was certainly true, but his mom might take offense if he agreed too strongly.

"I was on my way out, but first…" Joseph's mom turned to lock eyes on him with a serious expression. "I want Emily to hear me telling you to invite her to our house for lunch tomorrow."

He nodded again, though he noticed Emily's eyes widened at the idea. "I will invite her."

"On second thought," she said, "don't invite her, talk her into coming. I'll see you both tomorrow." She waved as she disappeared through the door faster than anyone could argue.

"Let me take some of this paper down," Joseph said. He felt suddenly fidgety as soon as they were alone and began to peel at some masking tape along the window.

"You're gonna let everyone see now?"

"Yeah, I guess. I thought you'd be more comfortable."

Emily squinted as though she had no idea what he was talking about.

Joseph wished he hadn't said anything. Emily hadn't known him very long. It had occurred to him that uncovering the window might reassure her that he had no intention of taking advantage of being alone with her. But if she hadn't worried about it, he didn't want to be the one to explain that he'd been thinking about something he wasn't thinking about because quite honestly, he felt guilty for thinking it. He put all his energy into peeling the tape faster.

11

Emily picked the sheet of brown paper off the floor and began to fold it. It was obvious that Joseph liked her. While that mostly made her feel good, his fidgetiness was contagious. She folded the roughly four foot square until it was wadded up no bigger than her hand, and then unfolded it enough to lay flat. She dropped that on the floor and followed Joseph to fold the next piece. They were going to need to talk to ease their nerves.

"This looks like a gym," she observed brilliantly.

"Yeah." He kept pulling off paper and raised his deep voice to be heard over the crinkling. "It's a place for families to come and be active together. I'll have classes for different ages of kids, with their parents, and we'll basically play games like a PE class at school. Only even more fun because it's not at school."

"That does sound fun," Emily said.

He dropped the last paper with one piece of tape still holding its bottom to the window as he turned to face the newly exposed space. "I sure hope I can convince enough people of that. I'm more worried about convincing parents so I need the kids to be excited enough to help talk them into it."

"The parents have to come?"

"At least one," he said. "It's important for two reasons. One... I just think it's important for parents to be that model of physical activity. And two... it's more cost effective. With the parents here to supervise, I don't have to hire extra adults to keep everyone safe. Though of course there'll still be a waiver."

"Could people sign up who don't have kids?"

"Sure. I expect it's more likely to have one parent sign up with two kids than the other way around so extra adults might help keep teams even."

She smiled at that. She couldn't be the only childless person interested in fun exercise. "What about when the kids are all in school?"

"What do you mean?"

"I mean are you only going to be open after school and weekends?"

"Oh, no," Joseph said. "I'll open at 6 am. The first hour of each day will be an open track." He took a few steps away from the window and gestured to some lines on the floor. "Right along here. The outside lane is for joggers, the inside for walkers. No sign-up required, just a drop-in thing so I'll expect more people when the weather's bad. Would you like to give it a try?" He held his hand out to invite her onto the track with him.

"Okay." Emily stepped closer. He held his hand out long enough that she thought he expected her to take it in hers. He dropped it to his side just before she reached out. At least thankful to have not embarrassed herself, she began to walk the track next to him feeling disappointed and very aware of her empty hand. It opened and closed awkwardly.

"I haven't finalized the schedule," Joseph continued, "but I also plan to have classes for preschool age kids later in the morning and maybe even something for babies."

"You're going to teach crawling?"

He rewarded her joke with a deep chuckle. "It'd mostly be for their moms, and it won't start right in January. Jessica will teach it.

She's not sure when she'll be ready, but she already sounds like she has good ideas."

"Glad to hear you have supportive family," Emily said. "I was getting the impression you intended to do everything here all by yourself."

"It's mostly looking that way. Though when I bought the building, I'd hoped... uh..." He lowered his gaze and glanced around uncertainly.

Joseph was so open and animated about his plans for the place that the abrupt shyness really piqued Emily's interest. "You hoped what?" she prompted.

"The one part I'm not excited about is the record keeping. You know, the class lists and financials and stuff. I knew it would take me a long time to open so I used to hope that by the time everything was ready I would... Well, I'll just say it. I hoped I'd be married, or at least engaged, to someone who would want to do that part for me." He still hadn't looked up again. "I know how selfish that sounds."

"No, it doesn't," Emily said. "I would love to do that."

Joseph's eyes jumped to hers. He looked briefly startled but mostly just amused.

Probably by the blush spreading across her face. Emily's propensity to say whatever popped into her head was a regular source of embarrassment. But it had never made her sound as though she was volunteering to be someone's wife on a first date. That was a new level of awkward. "What I mean is..." She chose her words carefully as she restarted. "Different people like different things, as I, for example, enjoy bookkeeping stuff that a lot of people find boring. So it is not selfish to hope your future wife might happen to enjoy tasks you do not. Like with my parents, my dad loves to cook and my mom really doesn't. He does most of the cooking and that makes both of them happy."

Joseph was nodding and obviously understood that she hadn't meant to sound so eager. He still seemed to be fighting a laugh, which was not helping Emily relax. She chose to move on. "Did you go to the meeting at St. Jude's last night?"

"Yeah. Everyone is on board with the new time. We'll be expecting you next week."

"You're sure it didn't bother anyone?"

"No," he said. "I mean, it didn't." They were still walking around the gym, and Emily noticed that he walked faster when he talked faster. "There were even a few new people. Newish. Some guy named Sean. Have you met him?"

Emily shook her head.

"I met someone named Heather. I guess she's only been there once or twice. Anyway, she sounded like the time change might help her come more often."

"That's good," Emily said. It was good. It also struck her that she wasn't bothered by Joseph talking about another woman. She didn't know if she was being mature or just odd to notice how his interest in Heather was plainly in growing the study group and nothing more. Either way, it brought to mind a recent incident when her thoughts went a different direction. "Who was the woman at the festival?"

He looked confused. "At the festival?"

"There was a woman who came up to talk to you when you were about to do the cake walk," Emily said. "She seemed to know you."

"Oh, right. Natalie." He looked at Emily for confirmation. "Blond? Kind of heavy?"

She nodded.

He winced. "Sorry. That wasn't the best way to describe her. She was just really skinny in high school so the difference jumps out at me. Anyway, her name is Natalie... it was Boyer, but I can't remember the last name of the guy she married. She teaches art at the high school now and wants me to hang the students' work in here in the gym."

Emily didn't have an immediate reaction to that. "Art in the gym?"

"I know." Joseph looked as though he didn't quite know what to think either. "It's not an obvious combination. And it sounds like it wasn't her first or even fifth choice location. But the idea is growing on me. I intended to keep the walls plain because I didn't want anything people would get tired of looking at. Natalie wants to come in to swap out the pictures on a regular basis and..." He jogged ahead, then stopped and spread his arms towards a back wall. "I was starting to think about offering this section right here."

Something in his eyes was seeking Emily's approval and made her hurry to catch up. But it also made part of her want to forget about art and walls and just walk into his arms to see if he approved of that. She resisted the startling yet highly appealing impulse to consider drawings on display. "A changing array of pictures in a gym," she said thoughtfully. "Like exercise for your eyes."

"Oh!" Joseph grinned. "I'm totally going to call it that. Not put up a sign or anything, but when people are walking by I'll be like don't forget to check out the eye exercise. And when Natalie wants to change it up, we'll be talking about the eye exercise. I know you were joking, but you've made it a thing."

Emily was flattered by the enthusiasm.

"And now maybe you can help me with my biggest problem," he said

"What's that?"

"You may have noticed that the walls need painting."

"You want me to paint?" she asked uncertainly, not because that was an awful thing to ask but because she didn't believe that could be his biggest problem. Joseph was a very capable guy with a big, supportive family.

"No, no." His expression shifted as he reconsidered. "Or actually, I wouldn't turn down the help, but... First I need to figure out a color." He turned back to the wall with his arms crossed and his brow furrowed.

"Oh." Emily copied his wall-studying stance.

Joseph smirked and put one hand under his chin to see if she'd do the same.

She raised her arm slowly, trying to keep her face serious as though she was giving the blank wall proper deliberation. They continued to cast sideways glances at each other though and the flirting kept her thoughts far away from paint colors. The only color on her mind was the red of his sweatshirt, which was at that moment her absolute favorite color. The way it stretched across his chest and bent arms emphasized that this gym wasn't only for other people. Though what she liked probably had little to do with the color. Those dark eyes would be just as attractive in a different shade as well. It was what was behind them that was so distracting.

Emily worked to force her mind away from Joseph and onto the question he'd posed. "What are your thoughts so far?" she asked.

His Adam's apple bobbed, and he drew in a long breath. It gave the impression that he was also pulling his thoughts away from somewhere else. "Not white," he said. "I don't want anything that boring. But I'm afraid anything too bright or bold will get old fast. And not too dark. That seems to rule out everything."

"Hmm." Emily dropped her arms and looked around. "Have you considered pink?"

"Pink?" His eyebrow inched up.

"I don't mean like fuchsia or anything that's a really pink pink," Emily clarified. "Just a pink tint. It would give the space a sort of healthy rosy glow that people might not even realize isn't just from the exercise."

"You want me to mess with people's heads?"

She shrugged rather than get defensive because he was clearly teasing. "That's not what I said."

"Pink," he said more thoughtfully. He turned in a slow circle. "A pink so light you don't quite know it's there except by the reflected... That's starting to mess with *my* head."

A smile tugged at her lips to see that Joseph was at least intrigued by her suggestion.

He started walking again and motioned for her to follow. "I'm going to let that sink in while I pick your brain about some other things." He pointed to the wall ahead, almost back to the front windows where they'd started. "My mom thinks I should put some coat hooks right here. I worry that's too far from the door to be convenient, but I can't put them on the windows so I'm not sure I have a choice."

"That's a good spot," Emily said.

"I'm not sure I'm sensing enough contemplation for something as important as coat hooks." His tone was scolding, but his expression was playful and more dominant.

"Well, how's this? People coming into a gym are probably not going to fret about a few extra steps. If they are, your classes will be a handful. And personally, I'd probably leave my purse with my coat, or by itself if it was warmer, and it would feel more secure farther into the room."

Joseph looked impressed. "I knew it was a good idea to get you in here." Then he winked, because it had been her idea. "But the consequence of proving yourself so smart is that now you have to take a look at my spreadsheets."

She tried to frown at this punishment when she was actually curious, both about these spreadsheets and how close they might have to stand to both see them.

"I'm beginning to work out a weekly schedule," Joseph explained. He pointed her towards a raised counter in the opposite corner. "I've had some responses to a survey passed out at the elementary school. Unfortunately, the one thing people have requested that wasn't on the list is ballet. I am not even remotely qualified to teach ballet."

"I took ballet for six years," Emily said, not because it was in any way relevant. He'd mentioned ballet though. She said what that made her think.

He stopped again and looked at her as though she'd just answered his prayers. "You can teach ballet?"

"Absolutely not," she said. "I'm about as graceful as a... a... I apparently don't even know what's graceful and what isn't. I was never very good, and it's been years. Having me teach ballet would be —"

"Inspired," he said.

She laughed in his face because even though she hadn't decided how to finish the sentence, she knew that wasn't even close.

"No, inspired," he said again. "That's the key word. If we call it a ballet-*inspired* class, everyone would know not to expect, uh..."

"Me to have any idea what I'm doing?"

He shook his head. "They'll know it won't start them on the path to becoming a professional dancer," he said. "But I'm sure you remember enough to put together some simple routines that would get the kids and parents moving. And the little girls can wear cute outfits, which you know is the only reason some of them want to take ballet."

Emily remembered a couple of recital costumes she'd been particularly excited about as a little girl. She'd always worn a pretty skirt over her leotard for practice, too. She couldn't deny his claim. Then she noticed how earnestly his eyes were boring into hers. "Oh, my goodness," she said. "You're not just teasing me about teaching this class, are you?"

"No." He seemed surprised that she'd thought he was kidding. "You don't work at Burger Brothers in the mornings. We could do a class of preschoolers one weekday and squeeze in some elementary kids on Saturday."

Just two hours a week? That would fit nicely into her schedule. And she'd been trying to think of ways to get more exercise. And she'd see Joseph while she was here. Was two hours enough? How could she go from you can't be serious to that sounds awesome without sounding flighty?

"Promise me you'll think about it?" he asked.

She nodded and secretly thanked him for the opportunity to appear reluctant.

"Great." He waved an arm for them to start walking again. "Now you can help me with the schedule and stuff."

Emily followed him behind the counter. There was a laptop and a bar stool. A second stool was against the side wall.

Joseph opened the laptop – it had a mouse plugged into the back of it – and began to open some tabs. "Oh, good," he said. "I got a few more responses. Sebastian helped me get the survey on the website. He does that sort of thing for a living so it was a lot easier than trying to figure it out for myself. Can I get your opinion on some formatting for this?"

There was a spreadsheet on the screen that Emily did want to examine, but she was distracted by the mention of Sebastian. She wondered if this was her chance to get the story on him.

"What's wrong?" Joseph asked. He'd looked up and detected either her question or the hesitation behind it.

"I wanted… Can I ask you about Sebastian without sounding gossipy?" She figured the ship had sailed as soon as the words were out of her mouth so she quickly tacked on some justification. "Things keep coming up about him. The first young adult group we were at together, he said something about his mom, something about how her struggles would never really be over, and I don't remember the context. I just remember everyone else nodded, and I didn't have a clue what he meant. A couple people seemed to be whispering something about him later. Then just this week, I mentioned Sebastian at work. Luke was asking about people I'd met, and he got angry just hearing Sebastian's name. He said his sister was married to a guy like that and I was like a guy like what, but he didn't elaborate. I'm really not trying to be gossipy. I just… I'm afraid of putting my foot in my mouth because everyone seems to know things that I don't."

Joseph gave her an understanding nod that put her at ease. He gestured for her to have a seat on the closer stool before he grabbed the other one and brought it over. They both sat at the counter but angled towards each other. His knee was nearly touching the side of her leg. He put both hands on his knees to lean slightly forward. When they were comfortable, he began to talk.

"I can tell you about Sebastian's mom," he said. "She's a recovering alcoholic." Joseph drew in a slow breath as he considered what to say. "This was mostly before I was born, but I know she got married and had two kids. I don't know if she was drinking before that or… It was bad enough when the kids were little that her husband became concerned for their safety. He left her, got custody of the kids, and moved away. I don't remember where they live now or if they're still… Anyway, losing her family apparently sent her into a downward spiral. She basically spent a few years as the town drunk. She lost her job and moved in with a guy who was also a heavy drinker. Then she got pregnant, with Sebastian. That was evidently the incentive she needed to clean herself up. By all accounts, she checked herself into rehab like the day she found out and has been sober ever since."

"But not without effort," Emily said, making sense of Sebastian's comment about his mom.

"Exactly. I'm sure it's... Opinion around town seems to be split between those who want to shun her for her past and those who admire her for overcoming it."

"And Sebastian gets caught in the crossfire?"

"Sometimes. I suspect it makes him an easier target for..." Joseph was speaking slowly. "But I don't think that's what makes Luke angry."

"Oh?" It was obvious there was much more to Sebastian's story, but Joseph seemed uncomfortable sharing the other part.

"I'm gonna tell you what I know," he said, "and what people say and..." He shrugged. "I'm afraid it's... murky."

"Murky?" Despite the rising tension, something about the word choice made her smile.

Joseph's lips pressed against a smile as well, then got very serious. "The comment about his sister worries me most, but I don't know anything about that. She might be someone who needs prayers."

Emily wiped the remaining smile off her face and waited to hear what she should pray for.

"Let's start with Luke," Joseph said. "If you don't want to put your foot in your mouth, you should probably know that he's recently divorced. It might not even be final. Word is she left him suddenly, and he's pretty much mad at the world now. With some cause."

"Thank you for telling me that," Emily said. "It isn't exactly my business, but it might help me be more sympathetic towards his attitude problems."

"Luke is a few years older than I am," Joseph continued, and his sister is a few years older than him so I really don't know her at all. But as far as Sebastian goes... there was an incident."

"An incident?" Emily was trying to be patient because she could see Joseph was uncomfortable talking about it, but drawing it out was making it worse.

"Shortly after high school, he was dating this girl named Kathy and apparently beat her up."

That wasn't what Emily expected at all. "Whoa!" she exclaimed.

Joseph held both hands up in a defensive posture. "This was about ten years ago, and I do not want to make it sound as though it wasn't a big deal. But people have been blowing it out of proportion ever since. I've heard people say she was in a coma for a week. I've heard people say he broke both her arms. I've heard... As far as I know, she didn't have more than a black eye. Please don't misunderstand me. I'm not saying that's okay. But rumors keep popping up about other girls without any evidence at all and... He and Isaac are friends. They've been working together for a couple of years now, and I cannot imagine my brother buddying up to a guy who goes around hitting women. That makes me inclined to give Sebastian the benefit of the doubt."

Emily worked to shrink her eyes back to normal size. "That's easy for you to say."

"What is?"

"I mean, it's easy to give someone the benefit of the doubt when you're stronger than he is." Between the biceps and the martial arts training, Joseph likely encountered few people with a physical advantage.

"You're right," he said. "And I would never fault a woman for avoiding being alone with him or anyone else, just in case. But that's not a license to malign his reputation left and right. I'm only saying try not to believe everything you hear."

"That's always good advice," she said.

He nodded. "Also, thank you for… Well, you seem to trust me enough to be alone."

"I can't help it," Emily said. She thought it was kind of a stupid thing to say, but it was the honest truth. Right or wrong, Emily couldn't help that she felt a protective vibe from him.

And stupid or not, Joseph seemed to approve of what she said. One side of his mouth lifted in a smile that drew her eyes and her thoughts to hopes of a kiss. Glances up told her that his eyes were also flickering to her mouth. She prepared herself to store this memory of their first kiss.

He suddenly smiled wider but groaned at the same time. "A real man would not dream of taking advantage of such trust." He seemed to be talking more to himself than her as he faced the computer and pointed at the screen.

Of course Emily wanted to be with a good man who deserved her trust. Of course. But she was still disappointed. "What are you working on?" she said, hearing far less interest in her voice than she'd had earlier.

"The weekly schedule," he said.

It was a mess. It was no wonder she didn't recognize what he'd already said it was. Emily quickly became absorbed in fixing his records. He had each class listed by a number and had to switch to a different sheet to see which number was which class. The schedule had 2 o'clock twice. There was a ton of unnecessary scrolling and she could see why he didn't like this part. He was making it so much more difficult than it needed to be. She enjoyed telling him all the ways he needed to improve his system. Oddly enough, he seemed to appreciate the chastising as much as the help.

She'd lost track of the time when he asked her if she was hungry.

The question may have triggered some rumbling in her stomach or merely caused her to pay attention to it. "I am a little hungry," she admitted.

"Good," he said. "Because I am, too. Do you mind if I run upstairs and grab us a snack?"

"Okay. I'm going to add some shading to these column headings while you're gone."

"More shading?"

"Trust me." She flashed a smile. "A prettier spreadsheet is also a more readable spreadsheet."

He laughed as though he was as amused as he was convinced. "I believed you when you said you liked this sort of thing, but, um…" Joseph dragged a hand over his face in an exaggerated attempt to erase the laugh. "Let's just say I believe you more now." Then he turned and walked away, presumably in search of food.

When Emily refocused on those rows and columns, they were a little prettier even before she made changes because of a feeling of contentment. Yeah, she was hungry. And yeah, she'd been sitting on a hard stool way too long. But Joseph was already making fun of her like they were old friends. He hadn't kissed her, but there had been indications that he'd like to. The day was encouraging. Also, she was having so much fun choosing a font for the days of the week that she kind of wanted to make fun of herself. "You're too narrow," she said to her latest option. "Oh, and you're just too… weird."

She made sure to stop talking to the font before Joseph got close enough to hear. He returned with a plate of chopped veggies and cheese cubes faster than he could have chopped veggies and cheese. "Did you have that ready?" she asked.

"Ready?"

"Already cut up and on a plate for in case I stayed so long I got in the way of your dinner?" Emily grew rather self-conscious as she formed the thought.

But Joseph nodded as though the interrupted dinner was the best thing that had happened to him in a while. He set the plate down with one hand and reached over to close the laptop with the other.

"I'm not –"

"You need a break," he said.

"Just let me…"

Joseph pushed the computer to a corner with a warning look on his face. It seemed he was telling her she was not allowed to do even one more thing. She was tempted to see what he'd do if she tried to lean past him to grab it. The thought of him physically stopping her made her face very warm.

She picked up a carrot instead. She liked carrots. Since trying to improve her diet, she'd not only lost some weight, she'd also been continually reminded of how many healthy things she actually liked. But not all of them. "You can have all the cauliflower," she said.

"Not a fan?"

She shook her head. "It's so tasteless."

"How do you not like something that has no taste?"

"I guess it might sort of… I don't know."

He smiled. "My mom doesn't like cauliflower either. So there won't be any at lunch tomorrow. Have you considered joining us?"

"You really want me to come meet your family already?"

"What do you mean?" he asked. "You've already met several of my family members."

That was true. What did she mean? "I guess I figured that since you didn't mention it right after your mom did that you were hoping I'd forget. Now I'm looking for validation that you either don't think it's a big deal or you don't mind if I interpret it as a big deal."

"I love the scary honesty," he said, eyes wide.

Emily slapped a hand over her face. Sometimes she did need to think a little before speaking.

"Can I say both though?"

She peeked at him between her fingers. "Both?"

"I can't say I understand the importance some people place on meeting the family." He attached air quotes with a mocking tone. "On the other hand, the idea of you attaching importance to it makes me more eager to talk you into coming."

She felt his hand very gently push hers off her face. The look in his eyes was more significant than any arbitrary relationship stage. This guy wanted to be with her, and he wasn't playing around. There was a pleasant flutter in her chest as she again anticipated a kiss. Then her mouth ruined the moment by spilling out some more unfiltered words. "You would not be taking advantage of me."

"So scary." Joseph's eyes dropped to the food and he turned slightly pink. "How do you feel about celery?" he asked as he crunched into a stick of it.

She liked it a minute ago. It was rather disappointing against her lips at the moment, but she went along with changing the topic back to food. It meandered through other random likes and dislikes as the two of them polished off the substantial snack.

Then Joseph jumped off his stool. "We've been sitting too long," he said. "Follow me."

Emily stood more slowly, stretching her legs as she began to walk across the gym after him. "Where are we going?"

"Just over here." He took his phone from his pocket as he spoke and tapped on the screen.

She couldn't see what he was doing over his shoulder. Though she was curious, she was also willing to wait for him to tell her.

He set the phone into some speakers against the opposite wall and turned around as a song started playing. It was loud but not so loud they couldn't talk over it. "Okay," he said, "let's see those ballet moves."

She only laughed.

"I'm not kidding." He waved a hand for her to get started. "You don't expect me to hire you without some sort of interview, do you?"

"I *don't* expect you to hire me," she said. "You're the one who said it was a good idea."

Joseph ignored her and put his heels together and his toes out. "This is first position, right?"

"You lied. You said you didn't know anything about ballet."

"No, I said I wasn't qualified to teach it." He pointed at his feet. "This is all I know, and this doesn't qualify me to teach anything remotely related to ballet."

Emily was going to say that was all she was qualified to teach, something remotely related to ballet. But she found herself distracted by the music. "What is this song?"

"It's the theme to *Ninjago*. Pirate mix."

"Uh…" She didn't even know what that meant. "Interesting."

"I know." He smiled at what she hadn't exactly intended as a compliment. "I've been collecting interesting music. It's going to be a popular feature here. Now stop stalling and show me some ballet."

"This doesn't sound like ballet music." Though it was rather catchy.

"That's another perk of a ballet-*inspired* class," Joseph said. "It can have more upbeat music."

"This class needs a name."

He raised his eyebrows questioningly.

"A ballet-inspired class is a mouthful," she said. "Maybe we could call it Ballet Moves. Then get the word inspired in the description."

"I like that." He nodded, then put himself back into first position with an expectant expression.

"Fine." There was no barre, but Emily moved closer to the wall in case she needed something to help her balance. She was amazed at how quickly some warmups she'd done as a kid came back to her.

Joseph followed along like a dutiful student. He was almost certainly more graceful than she was, which both impressed and irritated her. It felt good to move around after a few hours on that backless stool. Joseph's interesting music kept her entertained enough that she stayed relaxed. Part of her was simply having fun, but a bigger part was already imagining a whole class following her lead. They were four or five songs in when she asked Joseph if he had anything they could jump over.

"Something to jump over?" he asked. "Are there hurdles in ballet?"

"No." She paused to enjoy the confused expression on his face. "It shouldn't be anything that's difficult. Just some sort of markers so we can move in a circle and know where to leap."

"Hmm. I have some hula hoops."

"Too big," Emily said. "Little kids couldn't make it over the hoop and bigger people might... Just no."

"Jump ropes?" he suggested.

"Maybe. Ideally, the markers would be things the kids wouldn't be tempted to pick up and play with though."

"You're thinking like a teacher already," he said. "You're hired."

She smiled. "I still didn't say I would do it."

"You look like you'd enjoy it." He stepped closer. "Please?"

It wasn't fair to make him plead for something she was excited about doing. She only wanted a day or two to think about the class to make sure there wasn't something she was missing. Then again, what really wasn't fair was how hot he looked while asking. Emily's intention to keep thinking about ballet faded until her only thought was the feel of his lips on hers. She didn't have to imagine it. He kissed her again and again, a little longer each time. Soon her entire mouth was as involved as her brain. She'd been breathing heavy from the exercise, but it hadn't gotten her heart rate up nearly as much.

Emily kept her eyes closed as Joseph pulled away. She opened them in time to see a guilty expression as he glanced sideways. Towards the darkness outside the giant plate-glass window they were standing in front of. She didn't actually see anyone on Main Street, but she still understood exactly how on display their actions were. Emily felt guilty about the fact that she was more embarrassed about having been dancing in front of the window than about kissing Joseph in front of it.

"It's dark," she said to point out the obvious.

"It's November," Joseph said. "It gets dark early."

"True. But I probably should still go."

"And I'll see you tomorrow?"

She smiled. "Yes. Where do your parents live?"

"I haven't given you my number, have I?" he asked. "I'll text you their address so you'll have both."

The music stopped when he retrieved his phone. Emily found that she missed it while they exchanged some information. She put on her coat and gloves. Joseph walked her to the door and gave her a quick hug that was more effective at warming her up than the coat and gloves. Emily walked to her car, but on the inside she was still leaping and twirling.

12

Joseph moved the ladder out of the way. He slid the plastic along the floor before he moved the ladder to a new section in need of paint. Only about halfway done, he could already tell the color was perfect. It was a very pale pink. The paint chip Emily had picked out was labeled Sunrise Glow so he didn't think of it as pink but as Emily's Glow. It was just right.

The whole week had been just right. Emily had joined his family for Sunday lunch. His family plus Gabriel and Ella. They'd all talked and played some cards after they ate. As he and Emily left, she'd suggested that because Burger Brothers was only a few doors down, she could easily stop by on her way to work. He'd seen her every day since. She came over earlier each day and had helped him paint some. Now that it was Friday he would get to see her again at St. Jude's. In fact, they were going there together.

Joseph put away the paint supplies in time to get a shower and something to eat before he went out to wait by Emily's car. She smiled when their eyes met. He was definitely never going to get tired of the way she looked when she was happy to see him.

"I like that coat," she said.

"Glad you approve. My mom gives me a hard time about wearing it with casual clothes."

Emily smiled again as she unlocked her car. "As long as you're not wearing it to paint."

He let himself in the passenger side and got a whiff of hamburger and bacon as Emily joined him. Someone needed to bottle that scent. Emily drove quickly to the church. Or rather, she drove the speed limit, and they arrived quickly because the church was close. They hurried down the hall towards the sound of laughter. The room was about as full as it had ever been.

Gabriel and Ruth sat at the head of the circle, not that circles had heads. It was only the knowledge that they, though probably the youngest people in the room, were officially in charge. Ella was next to Ruth as usual. Gabriel's brother Eric had made it, as had Sebastian. Isaac and Jessica were there with their soon-to-be-born baby. Next to Jessica was a dark-haired woman Joseph didn't know. There was something familiar about her, which meant he'd likely seen her somewhere around town. Julia was there and Heather. Two empty seats were left between Julia and Sean, whom Joseph had met at the last meeting. He introduced Emily as they took those seats.

"Hope we haven't interrupted," Emily said.

Sean shook his head. "We haven't really started."

That seemed true as there were several conversations happening at once. They died down as all heads turned to Gabriel flipping open the notebook in his lap. He smiled and led the group in the *Our Father*, the traditional opening prayer.

"Quick announcement," he said as he finished. "We can't meet next week because it's the Friday after Thanksgiving and the school and church offices are all closed. I have to pick up the key from Mrs. Donnelly every week anyway, but she told me everything is closed like that was the final word. So we're taking a week off."

People nodded and shrugged at this news.

"Today we're going to talk about…" Gabriel gestured to Ruth.

"St. Thomas," she finished.

Isaac asked, "Which one?"

"The doubting one." Ruth gave Isaac a look of impatience as she gestured back to Gabriel.

"We read something about Thomas getting a raw deal with that label because so many of us have doubts." Gabriel glanced at his notes. "Questioning our faith is one way we can grow in it. Questions make us think. So our first question is… Can you think of a time when doubts helped you, when searching for answers brought you closer to God?"

Silence met this question. They usually started with some biographical information before jumping into questions. Perhaps he and Ruth assumed Thomas was well enough known since he was in the Bible.

Sebastian was the first to speak up. "Nothing monumental comes to mind," he said, "but there have been a few times when I read something or heard something in a homily that didn't make sense, and I felt better after digging a little deeper on my own than I would have if I let the question sit out there."

"I agree," Isaac said. "The church has such history that there probably isn't a question that hasn't been asked… and answered. It's a matter of knowing where to look."

"But those sound like academic questions." Jessica put a hand on her heart. "When you have personal doubts, when your faith is tested by hardships, there isn't an answer to that in a book."

"Depends on the book," Ruth said. She picked up a Bible from the floor next to her to illustrate her point.

"Psalms can be soothing," Ella said quietly.

"When you want them to be." Jessica tapped her chest again. "What about when you don't feel God? Where do you go when you question your relationship with him?"

Julia rolled her eyes. "It isn't about feelings. If you make it all about how you feel, then you start to sound like those offensive people who say you need to check your brain at the door to enter a church."

"No one has to choose," Joseph said. The idea that faith and reason were somehow at odds was a particular pet peeve of his. "We all need to experience God with the head and the heart. I think you can make the argument that most of us lean more towards one or the other and that's okay. But both are important. C.S. Lewis makes a beautiful analogy in *Mere Christianity* with the ocean. Standing on the shore seeing and hearing the waves and feeling the spray in the air is like an emotional encounter with God, like your personal relationship. And a map of the ocean is more like a creed. You need both depending on where you are in your journey, your life. Most of us have times, which I think Jessica was getting at, where the teachings of the church and even the things you read in the Bible just sort of feel like words on paper. That's when it helps to stick your hand in the water. On the other hand, admiring the view won't help you get across the ocean. That's when we need the map. If feelings are your only guide, you're not headed anywhere but relativism." Joseph's eyes landed on Emily as he finished speaking. She looked a bit awed.

"I need to read that book," she said.

Julia said, "Exactly my point."

Someone else said something at the same time, but Julia had their attention. "Feelings are irrational," she continued. "Following feelings gets us into trouble. It leads us towards doing what we want instead of what God wants for us."

"Doesn't God want us to be happy?" The new woman spoke up for the first time and sounded timid doing so.

"He wants us to find lasting happiness with him," Sebastian said, "not the kind of fleeting pleasures that all too often lead to addiction when they're not enough."

Julia nodded emphatically.

"I suppose it's like food," Isaac said. "If we judge by taste and don't bother to learn about nutrition, some of us would eat nothing but ice cream. Then we'd end up with diabetes and other health problems, which would certainly interfere with any kind of lasting joy." He gave Joseph a cheeky grin. "See, I can do analogies, too."

"It wasn't my analogy," Joseph said.

"And if I can be allowed to continue the food analogy," Emily cut in, "the ice cream tastes better when it's not the only thing you're eating. When you have a proper balance, using worldly pleasures the way God intended then... well, the ice cream tastes better."

Joseph wasn't the only one nodding. He'd fallen for a smart woman.

"You guys are making me hungry," Eric said.

After a laugh, Gabriel said, "Maybe we should get back to Thomas."

"Thomas?"

"Is that who we're talking about?"

"We got a little derailed there," Gabriel said, "but that's fine. It's a good discussion." He gave Ruth a nod.

"Okay, back to Thomas," she said. "He doubted the Resurrection until he was able to see Jesus for himself. But as soon as he did see Jesus, he said, 'My Lord and my God.' He recognized the truth instantly. So our question is... when was a time you failed to recognize a truth that was right in front of you?"

Emily raised her hand. "That's an easy one for me. I already told most of you how I spent years refusing to admit that I wasn't cut out to be a doctor and that I didn't want to work in a doctor's office period."

"I got one, too," Isaac said. "Jessica turned me down the first time I asked her out so she obviously spent some time denying this truth." He waved a hand between them.

"That's cute," Ruth said. "Unfortunately, I think people more often deny the truth of a bad relationship."

"Or the truth that even a good relationship needs work," Heather said. "Then they act like they don't know what happened when it falls apart after thirty years."

There was a pause in the conversation as it seemed that she was speaking from a personal place, and no one wanted to trample on it with another thought. She began to look uncomfortable with the quiet and added, "No one wants to admit when they're wrong," she said. "That's when we all deny the truth."

People nodded a little. Julia pointed at Ruth. "You're right about the bad relationship thing. I know someone who dated a guy longer than she should have because she was worried about hurting his feelings. It was worse in the end because she waited."

Sebastian nodded knowingly. "Honesty usually comes with fewer problems."

Heather suddenly scooted her chair away from him, as though she'd just noticed he was there.

"Okay, next question," Ruth said.

They discussed how digital altering had made it so people didn't always believe – and shouldn't always believe – what they see with their own eyes. And they talked about how things people see could be colored by past experiences. Overall, it felt like a more profound meeting than some they'd had, though they still had a few laughs.

Joseph and Emily helped rearrange the furniture when they finished. The group was expected to put the room back a certain way before they left. Heather came up to him as he was unfolding a table.

"Hey, Joseph," she said. "Don't let Adam hate me when he finds out."

"Finds out what?" he asked.

"I can't tell you. Sorry." She turned and fled the room.

Joseph reached over and tapped his brother. "Who was that?"

Isaac looked where Joseph pointed as the woman disappeared into the hallway. "Heather?"

"Yeah," he said. "Do we know her?"

"I think she's a friend of Kayla's. Why?"

"Just curious," Joseph said. Her being a friend of Kayla's did not bode well for whatever Adam was going to find out, but they probably couldn't do anything about whatever it was nor did he want to make it their business.

Isaac shrugged and grabbed a chair.

Joseph returned to Emily, who was frowning at her phone. "Did you miss a call?" he asked.

She stuffed it into her bag. "No one I need to call back right away. Are we ready?" She looked around.

"I think so," he said. They'd had enough practice that it rarely took more than a minute to move the tables and chairs. He waved to Isaac and Jessica as they left and then he and Emily said goodbye to the few others still in the room.

"Good meeting," Emily said on the way back to her car. "I still say it was super generous of everyone to change the time for me."

"And I still say it's not a big deal. Mostly because it was Isaac's idea."

She smiled at the fake pettiness and climbed into the driver's seat.

Joseph walked around the car wondering if he should bring up that phone call once they were alone. He didn't want to pry, but she'd seemed bothered. Though as she started the car, she only seemed bothered by the cold. She rubbed her hands together and her breath hung in a cloud ahead of her.

He reached over and sandwiched her hands between his.

"Oh, you're warm," she said. "Thanks."

She made no move to put the car in gear so he figured they had a minute to talk. And an excuse to keep holding her hands. "That person you don't need to call back right away," he said, "that wasn't anything... anything wrong?"

"Oh, no." She shook her head against the concern. "It's just this girl I knew in high school. We weren't even really that close then, and our lives have taken different directions since."

"How so?"

"Well... we actually knew each other from Sunday School. But she was starting to resent her parents making her go about the time I was wanting to go for myself. We butt heads a few times, which she seemed to think was funny and I, well, put up with. Then after high school... uh... She has two kids now, both girls. They have different fathers and the drama around it is crazy. One time she was going on and on about how the guys refused to call each other to coordinate their visits to take the girls off her hands at the same time. Another time she insisted one of the guys was planning elaborate outings and buying his daughter a bunch of stuff just to show up the other girl's dad."

Joseph sighed. "Those poor kids, caught in the middle."

"I know."

"What's the woman's name?"

"Savanah," Emily said. "She and I have had a surprisingly consistent pattern since we graduated. She calls me every four or five months. We chat a bit. She asks if I want to get together. I make some excuse. Then I don't hear from her for another few months. Honestly, every time I talk to her, I think it's going to be the last time I talk to her. Somehow, it never is."

Joseph guessed this woman called Emily whenever her regular

sounding boards got tired of her issues. He also figured that having a conversation a couple times a year was an annoyance Emily could handle. He moved on to asking her when he could talk to her again.

She smiled and pulled her hands free to begin the drive. The heater was beginning to warm up. "Well... your parents did invite me to come every Sunday and that's just two days away. More like a day and a half away."

"What about tomorrow?"

"I don't have to work tomorrow so I can't come over on the way anywhere." She bit the side of her lip in a cute puzzled expression.

Fortunately, she wasn't fooling him. They were way past needing an excuse to see each other. "How about you come over on the way to see me?"

That made her laugh. "What time is good?"

"Whenever you're ready to paint."

"Okay," she said. "I'll text you when I'm ready to watch you paint."

13

Emily looked out her window. There was still no sign of him. Her landlord was supposed to come over to fix her toilet. More importantly, he was going to show her how to fix the toilet.

She'd called Mr. Franks several times since moving in. Not only did he not act as though she was bothering him, he seemed eager for the opportunities to impart some knowledge. He didn't explain things in a way that said he didn't want her to call him but that he wanted her to have the confidence to handle simple fixes on her own.

His grandfatherly instructions made her wish her parents had taken more time to demonstrate rather than doing everything for her. She couldn't fault them though, at least not entirely. She'd never asked. She'd never bothered to consider that there might come a day when it'd be handy to be able to do things like flip a circuit breaker or use a plunger. Being spoiled became very inconvenient when living alone.

Mr. Franks was late though. He said he'd be over around one, and it was now just after two. Emily was going to have to tell Joseph she couldn't see him on her way to work. It was disappointing. They'd been seeing each other every day and would see each other again the next day, back at his parents' house for Thanksgiving. Even though it was disappointing, it felt healthy to be able to say their relationship would not fall apart because other things were going on one day.

Mr. Franks showed up within a minute of her sending the text. She didn't know how old he was. He was nearly bald and heavily wrinkled. But he seemed at least as nimble and active as her father. He apologized for being late, said he sat down for a moment after lunch and fell asleep. Then he asked her to lead the way to the toilet that wouldn't flush as though he didn't know exactly where it was.

He fiddled with the handle to confirm her diagnosis. Then he lifted the lid off the tank and waved a hand for her to come look inside. A chain had slipped off the end of a lever. He explained to her how the handle pulled on the chain to lift the flapper before he rolled up his sleeves and quickly put it to rights. He demonstrated a working flush. He told her that she could pour water directly into the bowl for an emergency flush and that some people kept empty milk jugs full of water for such an eventuality. All things Emily had not known.

She thanked Mr. Franks for his time and advice. Snow was falling when she showed him to the door. The huge flakes were melting as they hit the street but were already beginning to blot out the grass. He told her to be careful if she needed to go anywhere. She nodded, then put on a big smile as she waved. Thanksgiving was a day away and her list was ready and growing.

She stared out the window and spoke out loud to God. "Thank you for the care and concern of my landlord. Thank you for my parents' understanding that I still love them from my new path. Thank you for Joseph and the other friends I've met in Andauk. Especially Joseph. And thank you for this beautiful snow. The fat flakes are so pretty."

After watching for a few minutes, she checked to see if it was time to leave for work. It was only 2:30. Mr. Franks worked quickly.

She could still see Joseph. But she wouldn't be able to stay more than fifteen minutes. That sounded like just enough time to interrupt whatever he was working on. Even if it was a welcome interruption, she could handle not seeing him for one day. Was there something she could accomplish instead with only a small amount of time?

Emily considered calling her parents, probably only because she was holding the phone to check the time. She'd just talked to them the previous night. There had been no congratulations for hitting her goal weight, only admonishment that she not try to lose even one more pound. Her dad listened to her talk about teaching something like ballet to preschoolers and insisted there was a touch of pediatrician in her after all. She found the leap humorous rather than stifling.

Thinking of phone calls made Emily remember that she hadn't yet called Savanah back. There was a good chance she'd be at work in the middle of a Wednesday afternoon, a thought that made Emily feel guilty. She was thinking it was a chance to call her back without actually having to talk to her. If Savanah did pick up though, having to leave for work gave the conversation a hard stop time.

"Emily! About time you called."

Emily tried not to sigh audibly at the greeting. "Hey, Savanah, are you busy?"

"No, I'm at work."

That seemed like a contradictory answer, but Emily didn't question it. "Do you still work at the hotel?" she asked instead. Savanah was working as a housekeeper last time they talked.

"Yeah. Same old, same old."

"How're your girls?"

"They're great," Savanah said. "Doug's gonna take both of 'em this weekend to celebrate Harmony's birthday. Tommy'll be so mad when he finds out. He hates it when *his* girl spends time with Harmony's dad."

Emily only cringed in response. She didn't know what to say to someone who apparently relished the idea of making someone mad.

"It doesn't matter," Savanah continued, "because I have a date that night."

"Oh. You're seeing someone new?"

"First date in almost six months so it's about time."

"That's nice," Emily said.

"Hey!" Savanah seemed to have just gotten an idea. "You wanna get together so I can tell you about him?"

"I just started a new job," Emily said, "so I'm kind of busy figuring out the new schedule."

"Really? And do *you* have a new guy? Or any guy?" She snickered mockingly as she was constantly telling Emily she needed to date more.

"As a matter of fact, I am seeing someone."

"Ooh!" Savanah squealed. "Details."

"His name is Joseph, and he lives here in Andauk." Emily thought about what she could say without gushing, because she wanted to gush. "He's about to open a gym and wants me to teach a ballet class. And he is –"

"You're going to work for him?" Savanah interrupted.

"Not really. Just a couple hours a week."

"But it was his idea? Does he have lots of ideas?"

"Um?" Emily was confused by the disapproval she heard. The fact that Joseph was good at looking ahead was something she greatly admired. As excited as he was about being his own boss, he already had a few side jobs in mind in case he needed to supplement the income. "Planning is good," Emily said. "He wants to have a big family, and he wants to be able to afford a big family and still spend time with them."

"A family? Please don't tell me you're already thinking about marrying this guy?"

"I'm not thinking about marrying him *tomorrow*. But the whole point of dating someone is to see if he might eventually be someone I can marry so it makes sense to have that in the back of my mind from the beginning. I could easily call him my best friend and that's —"

"Ugh." Savanah interrupted with a gagging sound. "He's cute, isn't he?"

Emily smiled despite the rudeness coming through the phone because she pictured Joseph, and he was definitely cute.

"That best friend nonsense is just the hormones talking," Savanah said. "Trust me. You cannot even begin to consider getting engaged until the infatuation has worn off."

"What if that takes years?"

"Ha!" Savanah snorted. "I haven't been with a guy yet who didn't start to get annoying after a month."

Emily's first thought was that her parents could be awfully annoying, and she still loved them. Of course that wasn't the same thing. She didn't have time for a second thought.

"All I know," Savanah continued, "is that last time I talked to you, you were finally getting out from under your parents' thumb and now you're about to let some guy start running your life. Doesn't sound like an improvement to me. Great. Now I got somebody telling me I gotta get off the phone. You sure you don't have time to get together?"

"Probably not this week."

"Okay. Talk soon."

Emily wasn't upset that Savanah didn't give her a chance to say goodbye. She was relieved to have gotten the call off her to do list. She was a little upset by the conversation though. Was she letting Joseph run her life?

Emily thought about calling Julia next. Asking her opinion might help the friendship along. She didn't know Julia's schedule though, or if she might be somewhere she couldn't talk. A text would be better anyway since Emily only had a few minutes herself.

`Quick question: How do you know if you're letting a guy control you?`

The snow was still coming down, still not sticking though. Emily made sure she had her hat when she bundled up for work. If the roads looked worse in the evening, she could choose to walk home. She had a response from Julia by the time she arrived behind the restaurant.

`If you're asking then he is. Especially if you think he's cute.`

Emily stared at the reply without making much sense of it. The first part worried her. The second part made her want to discount the first, because what the guy looked like shouldn't matter. She stuffed the phone in her pocket to think about later.

Paula skated by as Emily entered Burger Brothers. The place was quieter than a typical weekday afternoon. The usual after-school crowd didn't show, likely because school was already out for Thanksgiving break. Only two customers sat at one table. It was where Paula was headed to check in.

Jojo was at the counter waiting for food. He gave an elaborate bow to Emily as she passed. She grabbed an imaginary skirt to curtsy in response, which made him grin from ear to ear. She hung up her coat and washed her hands.

When she walked up to Chip, he was wrapping a sandwich. He didn't acknowledge her presence. She was used to that type of greeting. The only other person in the kitchen was a gangly teenage boy named Aaron. He was very shy, at least around Emily. He returned her silent nod without meeting her eyes.

Chip passed the sandwich to Jojo. "You have enough layers for this weather?"

The older man again appeared to be wearing at least eight shirts, though possibly in a different order than the last time Emily saw him. She didn't remember that blue plaid on top. He tugged at the various sleeves of one arm with an odd expression of concentration. He might have been counting the layers or making sure they were all there. He gave a crisp nod as he took the wrapped sandwich from Chip.

Chip spoke sternly. "Eat that while it's hot."

Jojo gave no indication that he heard the last comment before he walked quickly towards the exit.

Emily waited until he was near the door before she asked about him. "He's not... homeless, is he?"

Chip shook his head.

"Does he have someone looking after him? Or does he need —"

"Lots of people in town look after him." He turned to Emily with a scrutinizing gaze. "I thought we might give you an important grilling lesson today, but I'm not sure how many customers we'll see with the snow."

Emily nodded with a weird guilty feeling. He had somehow made it sound as though the snow was her fault.

"Babysit Beethoven for now," Chip said.

"Yes, sir." Emily stood by the register expecting a slow afternoon. The register wasn't going to get into any trouble as long as she didn't touch it. A few people did trickle in. All of them gave updates on the snow. It was falling.

There was a familiar face in the early evening, a man with dark hair and eyes that cautiously swept side to side as he entered. There were no other customers in the dining room. Paula did a wobbly pirouette on her skates before she raced for the kitchen. It may have been Emily's imagination because Paula was always zipping around unpredictably, but it seemed as though she turned around the moment she saw Sebastian enter.

He walked up to the register, and his eyes searched the kitchen over Emily's shoulder before they landed on her. "Hi, Emily. How are you?"

"Glad to have something to do. It's not been real busy here." She put on her biggest professional smile. "So what can we get you?"

"Two standard hamburgers with fries, please."

"No drinks?"

He shook his head. "To go."

"Got it." Emily was getting pretty fast entering orders, especially when they were easy orders.

Sebastian paid but didn't immediately move to the pickup window. "You like it here better than your old job?"

"Definitely," she said.

"No problems? Other than having to learn new things, of course?"

"Well..." She glanced behind her to check that her boss wasn't close. The door to the cooler was open so she guessed Chip was in there. "Yesterday, I thought I broke the cash register."

"What happened?"

"You can see it's old. Apparently, the plug is really loose and will fall out of the wall if you don't regularly push it back in. No one told me that. Yesterday, it shut off while I was entering an order and I was like... What button did I accidentally push?"

Sebastian clamped down on a smile as he nodded behind her.

Emily jumped out of her skin to see Chip standing right at her elbow with his usual scowl. He pointed at Sebastian, then Emily. "You're going to wait because she's going to learn." He turned and motioned Emily to follow.

When she looked back, Sebastian gave her a smile and mouthed, "Good luck."

She followed Chip to the grill. He turned to her with a burger on wax paper in each hand. She hadn't seen him pick them up and didn't know how he'd done it so fast. She hoped she wouldn't be expected to learn that trick.

"Lesson one," he said. "These are burgers. We are going to cook them, not play with them. They are not to be flipped four hundred thirty-seven times." He dropped them onto the hot surface to much sizzling.

Emily nodded at his back and made a mental note to never flip a burger in front of Chip without asking permission first. He didn't say anything else, but he did look back occasionally to make sure she was watching. Then he asked if she knew what to put on a standard burger. She listed off the ingredients feeling proud, until she realized it was a rhetorical question. He was actually asking her why she didn't have the buns ready.

"Oh!" She grabbed some gloves and got to work.

Aaron was dipping fries into the oil.

Emily got everything wrapped up and into the bag. Sebastian didn't look terribly bored when she brought it to the window. "Hope that didn't take longer than usual," she said.

He shook his head as he took the bag. "Thanks, Emily. Have a happy Thanksgiving."

"You, too. Bye." She put her elbow on the counter and her chin on her hand as she watched him leave. There were no other customers in sight. She felt the counter tremble when Paula grabbed it to stop herself next to Emily. She was also watching the door close behind Sebastian.

"I hope he didn't notice how fast I went to the kitchen," Paula said. "I was going to try to keep Luke busy. Forgot he was off tonight."

Emily nodded as though she understood. She didn't fully understand, but based on Luke's reaction to Sebastian's name she could guess something of his reaction to the man himself.

"Oh, by the way…" Paula's tone changed dramatically as she turned an expectant face to Emily. "I hear through the grapevine that you and Joseph Ziebert are now an item. Is that true?"

Emily smiled her confirmation.

"Well done." Paula whistled. "That is a nice-looking young man and most definitely someone you can take home to mama."

"I agree," Emily said, though she wasn't entirely sure she did. Paula's comment gave her a weird panicky sensation that made no sense.

Chip's voice rang out and made both women turn around. "Executive decision," he said. "We're closing early. Aaron, go on home. Write nine on your time card and text me when you're home."

Aaron nodded and moved quickly to follow the order. He lived only a block away and walked to and from work.

"Emily, get your coat," Chip barked. "I'm going to follow you to make sure you don't slide off the road."

"You don't have to —"

He cleared his throat. "I'm saying jump here."

"Okay," she said. If the man was going to send her home early and make sure she was safe, she could let him be a grouch about it.

Emily walked through five or six inches of snow on the way to her car. She knocked her shoes together before she pulled her feet inside. The roads had been plowed but at least an inch had fallen since. There were a few tire tracks. Emily had less than a mile to drive so she wasn't too worried. It still made her a little tense in the dark. The falling snow could be mesmerizing in the headlights if she wasn't careful.

For some reason, she kept thinking about when Paula said

Joseph was someone she could take home. It was still bothering her. Emily's mom had given whole-hearted approval without even meeting him. Julia's doubts were confusing. And Savanah had accused Emily of exchanging one person's expectations for another. Was Emily jumping on board with Joseph's plans because that was easier than making her own? Or was she still just trying to do what her parents wanted by finding a guy who wanted to give them grandchildren?

The sudden and disturbing questions were pushed to the back of her mind as she parked in front of her house. Emily put on her hat and jumped out of the car, then waved to Chip as he drove past. She hurried up the sidewalk, sliding a little in the snow. It didn't teach her to slow down. She continued to rush to get out of the cold. Her foot slipped completely out from under her on the first step. Her knee came down hard on the one above it. Pain. Oh, so much pain. She wasn't sure she could stand up. She was afraid to try. She lay in the snow as cold seeped into the back of her neck.

14

Joseph drove slowly to his parents' house. The sun was bright and already drying the roads. Some people probably got time and a half for plowing on Thanksgiving morning. He hoped they were home now to spend the rest of the holiday with family or friends. Safety wasn't what made him drive slowly. He needed time to put on a thankful face, to prepare himself not to give anything away when everyone asked why Emily wasn't with him.

Mostly he didn't want to give away that he didn't know why Emily wasn't with him. That sounded bad. And he was afraid it was bad. Emily was going to come see him on Wednesday, but she'd said she had to wait for the landlord to fix something. That hadn't worried him. He knew she'd had problems there before.

But then she'd texted him last night with instructions to apologize to his parents for missing Thanksgiving. No explanation. It felt like a brush-off, which made the excuse about her landlord feel like an excuse. Two brush-offs in a row felt like she was putting off the day she said she didn't want to see him anymore. As if getting run over by a car would feel any better tomorrow than it would today.

There was a line of cars beside his parents' house. He recognized all of them. The Accord was Isaac's. The Acura belonged to Mr. and Mrs. Chadwick. Gabriel drove the almost thirty-year-old Bonneville and his brother another Accord. Ruth's little white

Escape didn't necessarily mean she was in the main house. She lived in the tiny apartment in the backyard.

Joseph remembered his six years there after high school, paying a nominal rent and saving for big dreams. It had started to seem that Emily was exactly what he needed to make those reality.

Joseph closed his eyes against those thoughts. Not thinking about Emily was the best way to get through the day. The last car in line was Adam's. If he had talked Kayla into spending Thanksgiving with his family, there might be hope for a lot of things.

Entering through the back door, Joseph stepped into the kitchen. It was warm and the smell of turkey roasting lifted his spirits. His mom and Gabriel's mom were standing in the middle of the room. They were dressed up and wearing aprons over their nice clothes. Mrs. Chadwick was holding a glass of wine as they chatted. The meal appeared well in hand.

Joseph's mom greeted him with a big smile. "Joseph!" she said. "Happy Thanksgiving!" Then her smile shrank. "Where's Emily?"

"She said to tell you she's sorry she can't make it. Something came up." He didn't have to admit he had no idea what the something was.

His mom seemed to sense it anyway. "Something came up?" she repeated doubtfully. Her eyes widened in a bid for more information. When he said nothing, she evidently decided – something Joseph could be thankful for – not to ask. "Okay. Go on and join everyone else in the living room for now. I may call you back soon because we'll need some muscle to get the turkey out of the oven."

Joseph nodded and moved to the next room. It was packed with people. He waved to the room at large to acknowledge some holiday greetings coming his way. And then came the questions. Ruth asked if Emily was with him.

"She's not coming," he said. "Something came up."

"I hope she's not sick or anything," Ruth said.

Joseph saw right through his sister. She wasn't showing concern for Emily, she was fishing for an explanation. He said, "Something came up," again and gave her a tight it's-none-of-your-business smile.

The only empty seat in the room was the middle of the sofa between Adam and their dad. "Hey, Adam," Joseph said as he sat down.

Adam nodded, but his eyes didn't leave the phone in his hand.

Having noticed Kayla was not in the room, Joseph was about to ask about her when he caught Eric shaking his head at him with a warning look. Apparently, Adam hadn't talked her into anything after all.

Isaac and Jessica were whispering about something in the corner of the room. It looked like an argument. All three of the Ziebert brothers appeared to be having varying degrees of trouble with women. Eric was fairly close and seemed like a safe person to engage in conversation. He might have been waiting for someone to talk to because he asked Joseph how everything was coming along with the gym.

That was a topic Joseph was always happy to discuss. He filled Eric in on some progress. Then he talked to him about joining his hapkido class. Though he hadn't progressed very high in rank, Eric did have some martial arts experience. It would be nice to have someone in the class who wasn't a complete novice. Eric did not seem completely opposed to the idea, but he didn't commit to anything.

Joseph's mom waved him into the kitchen after a bit. He went to remove the delicious-looking turkey from the oven. Then he stayed to help stack plates and carry dishes. It felt better to be moving around.

There wasn't enough room at the dining room table for everyone. Joseph sat in the kitchen with Ruth, Gabriel and Adam. Adam was across from him doing a fantastic job of ignoring everyone. Ruth was trying to do some matchmaking for Ella. She kept glancing into the dining room to make sure Eric wasn't listening. "Why won't you help me set something up?" she asked Gabriel.

"I don't get into Eric's business," he said. "Besides, I'm not sure I see them together."

"Why not? They're the same age. They're both really quiet. Same church. There's definite potential."

Gabriel shook his head and put down his fork. He also sent a quick glance into the next room. "Promise you won't say anything?" His eyes swept to the other people at the table before coming back to Ruth. When she nodded, he said, "I think he's interested in someone else."

"I thought you didn't get into his business."

"I don't. It's only a suspicion."

"Really?" Ruth leaned forward with interest.

Gabriel picked up his fork to indicate he wasn't going to say anything else.

Ruth stared at her food. "Well, I gotta figure out someone for Ella. She's great, but she's so shy I'm afraid she won't find anyone without help." She turned her eyes to Joseph. "I was looking at you for a while."

"You're looking at me right now."

"I mean for Ella," Ruth said. There was a tinge of annoyance because she knew Joseph knew what she meant. "She didn't think it would work, and I guess she must have been right since you seem to be hitting it off with Emily."

His sister was fishing again. There wasn't an actual question though so Joseph just went on eating.

Ruth huffed at the silence and decided to take it out on Adam. She elbowed him and said, "Why don't you put down the phone and join us?"

"I have nothing to say," Adam said.

There was an edge to his voice that Ruth ignored.

"Come on," she said. "What's wrong?"

"Nothing as far as you all are concerned." His eyes still hadn't lifted.

Ruth rolled hers and took a bite. "Stuffing is good."

"It is," Joseph said. He hoped they'd stick to talking about food. "Sweet potatoes, too."

Adam suddenly dropped his phone onto the table. "I guess you might as well know," he said. "Kayla is gone."

"Gone as in…?" Ruth's eyes were wide and a little fearful.

"Gone as in gone," Adam said. "The only reason I'm here is because she asked me not to be home when she packed." He picked up his phone and left his unfinished plate to return to the living room alone.

They all knew better than to follow. His departure killed any pleasantries about the food. Joseph was fine with the quiet. Not long after, however, there was some commotion in the dining room. They heard several surprised exclamations before Joseph's mom yelled, "Why didn't you tell us?"

Isaac said, "She wouldn't let me tell you until it was time to go." He was already in the doorway trying to usher Jessica through it. She was walking slowly with a pained expression on her face.

Joseph's mom followed them into the kitchen.

Isaac waved apologetically for the interruption. "Bye, everyone. We're on our way to the hospital."

"The hospital!?" Ruth said.

"Keep us updated." Their mom followed Jessica to the back

door wringing her hands. Then she turned back to those in the kitchen and said, "She was having contractions before they even came over and didn't say a word."

"Wow." Ruth smiled excitedly. "The baby's coming."

"Oh, I'm so nervous. I don't think I can eat now." Their mom returned to the dining room anyway.

Ruth and Gabriel chatted about something he was doing at work when the excitement died down. Joseph paid some attention. Eric slipped out with a brief wave as soon as he was done eating. Joseph decided to do the same. On top of his own worries, the day was proving eventful. He could not sit still any longer.

He intended to drive straight home, but Emily's place was on the way. He ended up stopping in front of it. Right behind her car. Emily was home. What if she really was sick? He needed to talk to her. He'd wanted to call her for hours but kept chickening out. If she was going to run him over, he didn't want to be the one to put the car in gear. He took his phone from his pocket with determination and a hint of something he hoped was not stupidity. She didn't answer.

"Hi, Emily. I missed you today and wanted to make sure you're okay. Please call me."

He waited a few minutes, just in case she only hadn't picked up in time. Had she seen his car outside? Was she deliberately avoiding him? If he thought he was losing it before, it was nothing to the current suspense.

Joseph returned to his gym, his sanctuary that had Emily's Glow all over it. Literally all over it. He threw some mats on the floor and began to work out. He went through every punch and kick he knew. Falls were better. He got to slap the mat with falls. The music was deafening, drowning out his fears of Emily, his anxiety for Isaac and Jessica, his grief for Adam. He worked until he was dripping, exhausted, and ready to face whatever came next.

He shut off the music and took his phone upstairs. It told him he missed a call from Emily, which made him realize he wasn't quite as ready as he thought. After a long shower, he felt calmer and less cowardly. It was time to hear what Emily had to say.

"Hi, Joseph." She sounded happy when she answered.

"Emily. Happy Thanksgiving," he said, which was a lame beginning. He wanted to let her lead the conversation though.

"Happy Thanksgiving to you," she said. "I'm so sorry I didn't come today. Were your parents upset?"

"Upset? Of course not. They were just... curious." Almost as curious as Joseph. "Is everything okay?"

"Mostly. I... yesterday was kind of awful because... Can I come over? Can we talk in person?"

"Yes. Please. I'd like to see you. But would you rather –"

"I'll be there in a few minutes," she said.

Joseph went back downstairs, unlocked the front door, and paced in front of it. It seemed to take more than a few minutes for Emily's car to pull up. And she didn't even get right out of it. It was like she was just sitting there letting him stew in the unknown.

Fears for the relationship turned to fears for Emily when he finally saw her because she was limping. He pushed the door wide to hold it open for her. "Oh, my goodness," he said. "What happened?"

"I forgot I'm a klutz and tried to run up some icy steps."

"You fell?"

She smiled. "I wiped out spectacularly."

He ran to bring his stools closer and helped her sit near the door. She dropped her bag on the floor and her coat on top of that as he claimed the other stool. Then he waited to hear the whole story.

"I slipped right in front of my house as I was coming home

from work last night. I thought I broke something because it hurt so bad. And I was afraid I was going to be lying there helpless in the snow for a long time."

"Were you?" Joseph asked. He was sure he went pale at the thought. "You should have called me for help."

"I had help," she said. "Chip actually drove behind me to make sure I made it home. I thought he had gone, but he just went down the street to turn around. He saw me on the steps when he came back." She laughed. "That man tried to be crabby even when he's being a hero. I'll never be able to take him seriously as a grouch again. He held out his hand and yelled, 'Keys!' I kind of threw them at him. He unlocked the door and carried me inside. Then he kind of stomped around while I called my dad. I convinced Chip he could leave me once he knew my dad – a doctor – was on the way."

Emily paused with a wince that didn't seem to be from pain. "That's when I texted you," she said. "I thought I should let you know that I might not make it to your parents' for lunch. I knew that, or I was afraid that, if I needed a cast I was going to be up half the night. But I didn't want to say I might not make it because I might have broken my leg because that would make you worry."

"And you thought telling me nothing would make me worry less?"

She smiled sheepishly. "I thought I would tell you more when I knew more. But then I forgot my phone. Or my mom did. She came with my dad when they came to get me, and she packed an overnight bag so I could stay at their place because it's closer to the... We didn't go to the hospital, we went to an urgent care place my dad sends patients to for x-rays. They were actually about to close, but my dad called ahead and got a friend to wait for us. And as you can guess since I'm walking on it, it's not really broken."

Joseph sighed with some relief. Only some relief. Because if this all happened last night, why had it taken her until four in the afternoon to fill him in? There was more to her story.

"I stayed the night with my parents, obviously. They were headed to my aunt's for Thanksgiving. I'm sure I could have joined them since it was family and all, but I didn't feel like being a surprise guest."

"How *are* you feeling?" Joseph asked with a nod at her leg.

"Oh, a little embarrassed at all the fuss actually. It's badly bruised and a little swollen but... I'll be fine. My dad's real cautious with painkillers so he asked me to try over-the-counter stuff first to see if that's enough, and I think it is."

"So you've been home alone all afternoon?" Joseph hesitated. "You could have..."

"I know," she said quietly. "But I'd already said I wasn't coming, and I kind of wanted to be alone with my thoughts."

That could not be good. Joseph had serious doubts that a woman could say she needed to think before delivering the news that everything was hunky-dory between them. But like an idiot, he asked anyway. "What did you need to think about?"

"Okay, bear with me." She splayed her arms like she was preparing to catch a beach ball. "My thoughts have been all over the place so this might not make any sense."

Joseph nodded and braced himself to be confused.

"It felt as though there were suddenly a lot of voices coming at me, mostly about you. My mom said she knew she would approve. My dad said you were great as long as you made me happy. And even Paula, at work, she said you were the kind of guy parents would appreciate. And I started to panic. I kept asking myself if that was why I liked you. Was I still just trying to please my parents? Was I looking for that approval?"

Emily took a deep breath. Her hands remained expressive.

"Then there was Savanah. I told you about her. I finally called her back yesterday, and she said... she said I just went from having my parents run my life to having you run my life, that it was like jumping from the frying pan into the fire. And I was thinking that I never would have come up with teaching a ballet class, or anything like it, on my own and..." She tilted her head apologetically. "This is the stupidest voice, and I don't even know what made me think of it but... Have you ever seen that old Rudolph cartoon with the elf who wants to be a dentist?"

"It's been years, but I'm vaguely familiar with it," he said.

"Okay. Well, there's a scene when Rudolph and the elf are both going to run away and one of them – I think it was the elf – he says, 'Let's be independent together.' It's supposed to be funny since that's not what independent means. Again, I don't know why it popped into my head, but I've been trying so hard to be more independent. I think that cartoon made this voice... like this super-feminist voice start yelling in my head like, 'You don't need a man to be happy!' Because my dad had said you made me happy, I wondered if..."

Emily stopped speaking abruptly and a slow smile spread across her beautiful face. "I was praying on and off about all this. And that's when I finally heard *my* voice. For the first time in my life I felt like I knew myself, I knew what I wanted. My voice said, 'Of course you don't need a man, but that doesn't mean you can't want one.' It said, 'Jumping into the fire is only bad if you don't love fire.' Right?" She looked as though she really wanted him to understand.

Joseph agreed cautiously. It was a fabulous analogy if he was the fire. But he wasn't 100% sure he was the fire. He waited for her to keep explaining.

"Just because I happen to do something my parents approve of doesn't mean I'm doing it *for* their approval," Emily said. "Just

165

because I happen to like some of your ideas doesn't mean I'm letting you control me. I'm making my own choices here, and I'm going to keep choosing you every day that I can."

There was fire in her eyes. Maybe they were both the fire. Joseph wanted to let her know he chose her, too. She'd already used enough words though. He stood up and put his arms around her, gently so as not to jostle her knee or knock her off the stool. He enjoyed holding her while his mind fit her into his plans, into all the places he'd been afraid to think earlier in the day. The gym would open in January, and she should be healed by then. A regular routine should be established by February. Valentine's Day might be a good time to propose. Emily could dictate how long the engagement lasted, but he wanted to make sure they were preparing.

His phone chimed from his pocket. He ignored it to pull back and kiss her. That was the only plan he needed at the moment.

Emily glanced down afterwards – she'd heard it, too – and he remembered that she wasn't the only person he'd been hoping to hear from.

"Just a minute," Joseph said. He smiled as he read the text aloud to her. "It's a girl!"

15

The bruise looked worse a few days later. A yellowish tinge was spreading around the edges. But it didn't hurt as much. She'd been a little worried that work would be awkward after Chip's rescue. He acted as though nothing had happened. He even glared at her when she didn't hobble fast enough so everything was normal there.

Joseph's gym, which she was trying to convince him to name Joseph's Gym, was beginning to feel like a second home. More importantly, all of Andauk was feeling like home. Emily didn't feel like the newcomer anymore. She was one of them. She was even included in the young adult pre-meeting meeting. It wasn't a real meeting or even a pre-meeting. It was only a joking title for the fact that about half the members of the group spent Sunday afternoons at the Ziebert house.

Emily came with Joseph. He was an early riser and normally attended the earlier Mass. He made it sound like no big deal to switch to the later time to go with Emily. In fact, he sounded happy that she let him pick her up and take her to church on the way to his parents' house.

He opened the back door for her and smiled patiently as she stepped inside somewhat inelegantly. There were only two steps, but she went up lopsided because she still preferred not to bend the injured knee more than necessary.

Mrs. Ziebert was in the kitchen. "Emily," she said, "it's nice to see you again. I... Are you limping?"

"Just a little," Emily said.

"What happened?" Her eyes widened. "Is this why you couldn't join us for Thanksgiving?" There was concern in her voice but relief in her eyes.

"Pretty much," Emily said. She was as happy as anyone to pretend her thoughts hadn't been as banged up as her knee. "I slipped on some ice, and my dad took me for an x-ray to make sure nothing was broken."

"Oh, dear. But you're okay?"

Emily waved away the sympathy. She was afraid it highlighted the clumsiness that caused the injury. "It's really not that bad."

Mrs. Ziebert looked past her to Joseph. "Get her in the living room so she can sit down."

"Yes, ma'am," he said, with only a hint of mocking.

Emily felt his warm hand on her elbow as he led her through to the next room. He wasn't supporting any physical weight, but she still felt lighter when he touched her.

Joseph's dad was sitting in a recliner in a corner. Ruth was sharing the sofa with Gabriel and Ella. There was noticeably less space between her and Gabriel than between her and Ella. It appeared Isaac and Jessica had not changed their minds about skipping a week. Emily understood since they'd only returned home from the hospital the previous day. She was still disappointed not to see the new baby in person. Joseph had visited and shown her pictures.

"Are you limping?" Ruth asked.

Joseph deposited Emily on a smaller loveseat and joined her on it at the same time.

"I slipped on some ice," Emily said. "I'm fine though." She

mostly wished people would stop asking. A small part of her was glad they noticed though because it might mean her regular gait wasn't as ungainly as she thought.

"Any chance we'll be seeing Adam today?" Joseph asked.

His attempt to change the subject was obvious. It made Emily smile that he knew she was tired of talking about her injury.

Ruth shrugged at him.

"Your mom just texted him to find out," Mr. Ziebert said.

Joseph acknowledged that with a nod. "Did he say anything else after I left on Thursday?"

"Not a single word." Ruth's expression suggested there had been plenty of tension with that silence.

Weird clattering noises and exclamations from the kitchen caught everyone's attention. Mr. Ziebert leaned forward in his chair. "Do you need a hand, honey?"

"No," she called, "I got it." After a bit more clattering, Mrs. Ziebert appeared in the doorway shaking her head. "I knocked some stuff out of the cupboard, but it was all plastic so it's fine." She sat with a sigh, then pulled her phone from her pocket. "Is there anyone here who hasn't seen pictures of my first grandbaby?"

There was some amusement at her enthusiasm and reluctant head-shaking.

"Gabriel?" she asked hopefully. There was already a picture on her screen.

"Ruth showed me some," he said. "And my mom showed me the ones you sent her this morning."

"Emily?" Mrs. Ziebert turned an eager face on her.

"Joseph only showed me a few," Emily said, "so I may not have seen *that* picture of your new grandbaby."

Mrs. Ziebert beamed and stood up at the same time as Emily. They met in the middle of the room to agree on exactly how adorable the newborn was. Ella got up to get a better look. Joseph tipped his head to glimpse the baby through the group. His mom scrolled through several closeups that all looked very much the same. The baby was so tiny and precious with her face bunched up in sleep that no one minded.

Then she came to a picture that made everyone pause. Jessica was sitting in a hospital bed looking up at Isaac. He was leaning over her with his new daughter wrapped protectively in his arms. Love and joy radiated from the captured moment. It was a fitting finale to the show. After a few moments of appreciation, Mrs. Ziebert lowered her phone and the younger women returned to their seats.

Joseph greeted Emily's return by giving her hand a quick squeeze.

The peace was disturbed as Mrs. Ziebert saw something on her phone before she put it away. Her mouth dropped open in a silent gasp. She set it face down next to her looking for all the world as though she'd been physically wounded by the small object. Emily looked quickly away. It wasn't her place to ask.

Joseph had noticed as well though. "Mom, what's wrong?" he asked.

"I... uh..." She glanced at the phone, still visibly shaken. "Adam won't be coming today."

"What did he say to you?" Joseph pressed. A simple no thanks would not have upset her so much.

She fidgeted a minute, wringing her hands, then said very matter-of-factly, "He suggested that continuing to ask every week would be a waste of my time."

An uncomfortable silence followed, during which Emily couldn't help but imagine a number of offensive ways such a suggestion might have been worded. To his mother. She sensed that Joseph was distressed by similar thoughts.

"He's hurting right now," Mr. Ziebert said. "We'll need to give him time."

"Okay." Ruth clapped her hands suddenly. "This feels like a good time to vote. And change the subject."

"Vote on what?" Emily asked. She sent Ella an apologetic look as it appeared she'd cut her off before she could ask the same thing.

Ella just turned expectantly to Ruth. She was eager to follow her in this confusing but hopefully less personal direction.

"Gabe and I have two ideas for saints to discuss next Friday," Ruth said. "Since we have three members here, we can vote without worrying about a tie."

"Which saints?" Emily asked.

"Saint Eloi or Saint Anthony of Padua?"

"Is that the St. Anthony that, um…" Ella looked at the carpet while she found the words. "The one who helps with lost things?"

"Yes," Ruth said.

"Let's hear the campaign speeches." Joseph gestured for Ruth to begin.

She narrowed her eyes at her brother.

"You want informed voters, right?"

She sighed. "Fine. I thought we could discuss St. Eloi because he was a wealthy man who dressed in expensive clothes with a nice house and everything but also used his money to aid those in need. It seems like a good jumping off point to talk about things, like money or technology, that are not inherently good or evil but can be used for either. We haven't worked out specific questions yet. And Gabe –"

"Can speak for himself," Joseph interrupted.

Ruth rolled her eyes.

Gabriel smiled at her. "I suggested St. Anthony. Something we read talked about how he was something of a rock star preacher.

It said he spoke in front of huge crowds and sometimes had bodyguards because people wanted to try to cut off pieces of his clothing as relics."

"Wow," Ella said.

"I don't know what that has to do with lost things," Ruth said.

Gabriel shrugged and continued, "We haven't worked out details on him either, but that made me think we could have questions about both the power of inspirational speakers within the church but also the dangers of giving them too much power. Of being swayed by pretty words without thinking about real truth that may or may not be behind those words."

"Those are both good ideas," Emily said.

Joseph nodded in agreement.

"Let's just do both," Ella said.

"Yeah," Emily said.

Joseph nodded again and added, "One this week and one next."

"Okay." Ruth glanced at Gabriel, who seemed to be on board with the plan. "Who wants to do St. Eloi this week?"

Three hands went up, though only half-heartedly. It was more like they were waving at each other than casting votes.

"Oh, wait," Gabriel said.

Ruth winced in sudden guilt. "You all would have voted for his if I said it first, right?"

The expressions around the room confirmed this.

Gabriel shook his head before anyone said anything. "No, that's not it," he said. "But I need a calendar."

Ruth tapped on her phone a couple times before she held it in front of him.

"Perfect," he said with relief. "We'll have three Fridays in December so on the last one –"

"No." Ruth cut him off sharply.

Ella chuckled as though she knew what that was about.

"Come on," Gabriel said. "It would be fun."

Ruth rolled her eyes dramatically as she turned away from him and towards Joseph and Emily. "Gabe has this ridiculous idea that... Do you know the song Good King Wenceslas?"

"Sort of," Emily said. She knew she'd heard it at some point.

"I think I only know the first verse," Joseph said slowly. His head seemed to be nodding to imaginary lyrics. "Actually, I'm not sure I know the entire first verse."

Gabriel looked serious. "You're missing out."

Emily took out her phone to look up the lyrics.

Ruth sighed loudly enough to hear across the room. "It's a really old song," she said. "The words are old English and Gabe thinks we should talk about St. Wenceslas and maybe St. Stephen – because he's mentioned in the song – and anyway, he wants to do the meeting with everyone trying to speak like that the whole time. With thee and thou and yonder and whatnot."

Ella was still stifling some giggles.

The words on Emily's screen made her smile. She was pretty sure she couldn't talk like that but might be entertained watching others try.

"I'm not doing it," Ruth said.

"Isaac might play along." Joseph tilted his head thoughtfully.

Gabriel frowned. "Eric wouldn't."

"Who else might be there?" Ruth asked.

"Julia," Emily said. She didn't know her well enough to guess how she'd feel about the idea.

Ruth's eyebrows shot up. She looked at Gabriel. "Eric and Julia?"

He held up a hand. "I'm not saying anything."

"What about Sebastian?" Ella said. "He's usually there. Would he participate in…"

Ruth reluctantly turned her attention from Gabriel. "I don't know about Sebastian. Who else can I get on my side?"

Ella shrugged, but she said, "I don't see Heather doing old English."

"Heather." Joseph said her name as though it reminded him of something.

Emily gave him a questioning look.

"I just remembered she said something about Adam at the last meeting," Joseph said. He shook his head. "It's not important now."

Emily turned her thoughts back to Ruth and Gabriel's playful argument. "I think your idea might depend on the mood of the evening," she said. "I'd be bad at it, but I'd give it a try if everyone else seemed to be having fun."

"Light questions," Gabriel said as though making a mental note.

Ruth sighed again. "Don't help him."

"If the rest of us are enjoying it," Joseph said to Ruth, "I bet even you will be throwing out yon old school jargon."

Gabriel cringed.

"At least I won't be the only one bad at it," Emily said.

She felt Joseph nudge her shoulder with his. "Hey," he said.

She didn't try to hide her laugh.

"I see what you mean," Ruth said drily. "You make it seem so fun to sound like an idiot."

Joseph pulled a couch pillow from behind his back and threw it at his sister.

She caught it. Then she stuck her tongue out at him.

"Well…" Mrs. Ziebert stood up. "I need to check on lunch. It should only be a few minutes. But from what I'm hearing, this young adult group seems to be working out pretty well."

"So far so good," Ruth said. "However... Isaac will be thirty in like two months. Will we have to kick him out when he's an old man?" She waved the pillow at Joseph, indicating he might be wishing he still had it available. It was clear she had no interest in kicking anyone from the group – which was officially for anyone in their 20s or 30s – and only wanted an excuse to call someone about to turn thirty an old man.

Joseph made a mildly threatening move that didn't fool anyone.

"Well, actually..." Emily had a different concern. "Will he and Jessica still come with a baby? Or will they have to take turns staying home with her?"

"No," Ruth said adamantly. "I already talked to Isaac, and he promised me they would keep coming at least until she can crawl. Then it might –"

"Hello! Grandmother right here." Mrs. Ziebert had stepped into the kitchen but popped through the doorway as she spoke. "I will be available for babysitting on Friday nights."

"How many kids are you willing to watch?" Joseph asked.

Most of the eyes in the room jumped to Emily's face at the question. It was well-known in his family that Joseph wanted a big family. Emily could feel them trying to measure her reaction. But it was only curiosity and not expectation that she felt. Part of her wondered how much of her parents' interest actually carried expectation. Regardless, knowing her own mind on the subject freed her from real or imagined pressure. She responded with a calm, impervious smile.

Joseph realized he'd been at least partially misunderstood. "What I meant," he began to clarify, "was what you'd think about watching kids of members who are not related to you."

Ella made a noise like a cross between a cough and a snort. "If you're looking at me, I'm afraid it'll be a long time before anyone has to cross that bridge."

"I'm working on it," Ruth said, "but you're not helping."

Ella narrowed her eyes at Ruth while fighting a smile. Emily interpreted that to mean Ella liked the idea of her friend helping with her love life but didn't want to admit it.

"Well, you or any of the members who might start having kids while still considering themselves young adults," Joseph said. He turned back to his mom. "If we could get permission to use another room at the school for childcare, would you help?"

Though she nodded, she looked skeptical. "That could be an ambitious project."

Joseph looked thoughtful. "We would need two adults if it was at the church, plus a backup. But it sounds like we have some time to figure it out."

He was planning again, thinking about the future. Emily admired the quality rather than seeing it as controlling. She knew he'd consult her as they moved forward. Even more importantly, she knew it was her decision to move to Andauk that had let her cross his path in the first place. He hadn't pulled her in. She had taken the first step into his plans. She wasn't drifting anymore.

www.ingramcontent.com/pod-product-compliance
Lightning Source LLC
Chambersburg PA
CBHW031352170626
46807CB00002B/935